TRBe

Jonno Joins

T. M. ALEXANDER

PICCADILLY PRESS · LONDON

T. M. Alexander likes short words more than long ones and spinach more than cabbage. She writes in a little room hidden away behind a secret door that's disguised as a bookcase. If the door ever gets stuck she will never be seen again.

Tribe: Jonno Joins is her first book.

Get to know the Tribers at www.tribers.co.uk

Contents

For Otter, Wib and Boo

First published in Great Britain in 2009
by Piccadilly Press Ltd,
5 Castle Road, London NW1 8PR
www.piccadillypress.co.uk

Text copyright © T.M. Alexander, 2009

A catalogue record for this book is available from the British Library.

ISBN: 978 1 84812 026 6 (paperback)

1 3 5 7 9 10 8 6 4 2

Printed in the UK by CPI Bookmarque, Croydon, CR0 4TD
Cover design by Patrick Knowles
Cover illustration by Sue Hellard

Mixed Sources
Product group from well-managed
forests and other controlled sources
www.fsc.org   Cert no. TT-COC-002227
© 1996 Forest Stewardship Council
FSC

Jonno
Joins

day one of the summer term

You never know what's round the corner. My mum says that all the time.

When I was small, I used to think she was giving me a warning. I thought she meant that you should watch out in case you turn a corner and get caught up in the middle of an army of purple aliens clambering back on to the mother ship, and disappear FOREVER. Even though I thought it was unlikely, I would find myself slowing down e v e r s o s l i g h t l y at corners until I had a proper view ahead. As soon as I saw the coast was clear, I'd speed up again. I don't do that now of course, because I understand she means that you never know what's going to happen next. It's not about luck or un-luck because Mum says it when someone's won the lottery *and* when

3

someone's died. It's just a fact.

And the fact of my story is that something's come round my corner and all of a sudden I'm part of it, and it feels important, so I'm keeping a record of how it started.

Actually it began with a kind of alien – a new boy. I expect our teacher (she's called Miss Walsh) introduced him and told us to be nice and all that, but if she did, I didn't take any of it in. Don't get the wrong idea, I'm actually a bit of a nerd, but I only listen to the interesting bits. The in-between stuff that teachers like to say but *I* don't need to hear gets separated off and binned, like junk mail. I don't even know where Newboy sat that first morning, except that it wasn't anywhere near me.

At break my mates and I raced outside to get on with whatever it was we were going to get on with. Our territory is in the corner by the netball court where the trees hang over. It's a scrubby bit of dirt really – the shade kills all the grass – but it's ours so it's good anyway.

There are four of us. I'm Keener. There's Copper Pie (funny name, I know). Next there's Fifty and, last but definitely not least, there's Bee. (Not a cool thing to admit but yes, I am friendly with a girl.)

The four of us didn't exactly *choose* to be mates. But when you've known someone since you were four years old, they sort of stick whether you like it or not.

It was sticking that I first remember us doing. Fifty's mum had come in to school to help us make papier-mâché balloons. Bad idea. Fifty's too-sloppy newspaper kept sliding

4

off. Copper Pie burst at least three balloons by pressing too hard. Bee knocked over the glue diving to save the slippery balloons. By tidy-up time, there was more goo on them than anywhere else. (None on me though – I borrowed the yellow rubber gloves meant for wash-up time because I didn't like it.) I remember all the laughing and thinking that school was nice, which it was in Reception.

We've been put in the same classes ever since and never bothered to make any other friends. We don't need anyone else.

We *especially* didn't need anyone else in our patch. At breaktime Fifty was the last of us to step under the tree, followed by someone else. The sun stopped me seeing who it was. I wasn't worried. Other kids *are* allowed to come and talk to us, although hardly anyone does. But as the boy-shape moved forwards into the shadows, I could see it wasn't someone I knew. And strangers were NOT welcome. Without saying anything, we all turned away and tried to carry on as usual, but he didn't leave. We could all feel him watching us.

Copper Pie spoke first. 'D'you want something?'

The shape shrugged.

He tried again. 'I said, "D'you want something?"'

'Not especially,' said the shape.

'Go away then.'

We're not meant to speak to people like that at school. There's a motto: We don't all have to be friends, but we all have to be friend-ly.

'I'm fine here,' said the stranger, who I worked out must be Newboy.

I really wanted to get rid of him but I didn't know what to do. Most people we know would have scuttled away if Copper Pie told them to. (He can be a bit of a thug.)

Fifty tried next. 'Listen, you're new so you don't know, but this is *our* area.' He used the I'm-so-charming smile that works with the teachers. He practises it in front of the mirror, in every window, and on the back of shiny spoons.

'Says who?' said Newboy.

'Says me,' said Fifty, looking straight into Newboy's armpit.

I could see that a midget telling him to get lost wasn't going to work. But Newboy seemed *so* unbothered it was difficult to think what *would* work.

Bee put one hand on her hip, pointed at the stranger and tried her favourite saying – with the American accent and *all* the actions.

'*You're* invading *our* personal bubble.' She drew an imaginary line round the four of us with her finger, then put her hand back on her hip and flicked her very long black fringe out of her eyes so she could stare at him.

He shrugged and stayed exactly where he was.

And so did we.

We hung around and talked in quiet voices but it was totally fake because all the time HE was leaning against the trunk of OUR tree working his heel into the ground, making a hollow. I'm sure all the others felt like me: mad. I wanted to shout 'Go away' but I didn't dare.

Usually break is too short but on that day it was too long. We couldn't leave our patch and play somewhere else because we had to protect it. We couldn't carry on as normal because of *him* lurking. I suppose we could have shoved him off but me and Fifty aren't like that, and Copper Pie *is* like that but is trying not to be. And Bee, well, she's used to people doing what she says, but Newboy didn't know that.

At last, the bell went and we lined up.

'What did he think he was doing?' I asked.

'No idea. Must be a weirdo,' said Copper Pie.

'Well, let's hope he decides to be weird somewhere else,' I said.

'We'll make *sure* he does,' said Bee.

Bee's always like that – definite. She's never 'not sure' or 'can't decide'.

'How are we going to do that?' I was thinking force fields, trip-alarms, perimeter guards.

'Make him not *want* to come near us,' she answered, with a mean look.

'Scary. I like it,' said Fifty. 'It's time to make Newboy's life a living hell.'

getting rid
of Newboy

It didn't take long for the campaign to start. In history (we're doing Romans), Fifty was sitting in front of no-name Newboy. He put up his hand. 'Please Miss Walsh, I'm finding it difficult to concentrate because someone behind me keeps kicking my chair.'

Lies. *Good move*, I thought. Unless Lily had grown stilts, there was only one pair of legs that could be guilty. Newboy didn't get a full-blown telling off – after all, it was his first day – but it showed him we meant business.

At lunch, I was confident Newboy would decide we weren't worth the bother. We demolished sausage, peas and jacket potato and headed for our spot and can you believe it? He was there. Sitting cross-legged on the ground with his back to us, picking at the bark of the biggest tree – our bark, our tree.

An open declaration of war if ever there was one.

I'd like to say we were up for it but I think we were all a bit . . . not scared but . . . confused . . . about what to do next. Generally kids don't act like Newboy – they find someone who doesn't *mind* playing with them.

We hovered for a minute nearby. Copper Pie kicked the ground a few times, sprinkling dirty specks over the back of Newboy's white T-shirt.

He twisted round so that I could see one of his eyes. 'Hi.'

Not one of us answered.

I waited to see what was going to happen. Hoping there wasn't going to be a fight.

'Let's just go somewhere else,' said Bee quietly.

Phew! My thoughts exactly.

'No way,' said Copper Pie loudly. He walked round so he was facing Newboy and stopped with the toe of his trainer actually touching the skin of Newboy's knee. Newboy did nothing.

'Let's show the newbie —'

'No. Let's not show anyone anything,' I said quickly.

'Same,' said Fifty. (He can't say 'I agree' like normal people.)

Bee yanked Copper Pie's arm and dragged him away. We all try and keep him out of trouble. It isn't always easy.

'Go find yourself some other kids to hassle,' she shouted.

'Loser,' Copper Pie added on the end.

Newboy didn't look up. He didn't even stop flaking the lumps of loose bark off the tree. I couldn't help thinking that if there was a loser round here, it wasn't him. Although leaving didn't seem right, none of us wanted to spend another breaktime with the limpet boy.

'He's probably got something wrong with him,' said Fifty. I hadn't thought of that. I glanced over to check. It was almost like he knew I was studying him because he shifted round a bit and we accidentally locked eyes (or glasses in his case). And he smiled a big friendly smile. It was almost impossible not to smile back but, by whipping my head back quickly, I managed. It was very creepy. I had expected a glare.

'What's wrong with him is the fact that he's a cling-on,' said Bee, leaning against the wall by the loos. 'We need a plan to lose the stalker, and the first part of it has to be to get outside before him.'

'Agreed,' said C.P. 'Then we'll have the advantage.'

'But we need to stop him from following us . . .' said Fifty.

'A blockade,' I said.

'Made of what?' asked Fifty.

'We could rope off our area, tie one end to the branches and put the other through the wire fence.'

There was a general lack of enthusiasm for my idea. Not unusual.

'He'd climb under,' said Fifty. 'What about a fire?'

We always ignore anything he says that's to do with fire. It's an unhealthy obsession (according to his mum) and scary (according to us).

'We could make a really bad smell,' said Copper Pie.

'You don't need us for that. You could do it on your own,' said Bee.

'Sandbags,' I said.

'Get real, Keener.' Bee has lots of expressions she uses to diss people.

'Right, everyone think. It needs to be something *we* can get past but stops *him*,' said Fifty, spelling out the problem.

'Bodies,' said Copper Pie.

Fifty made an excellent you-total-idiot face. 'What?'

Copper Pie said it again. 'Bodies. We've got four. He's got one. We make a human wall, like in football.'

Fifty quickly changed it to a you're-not-as-stupid-as-you-look face. 'You're not as stupid as you look,' he said. 'What does everyone else think?'

'It *might* work,' I said, not very keenly. I didn't fancy getting into a scrap.

'Right, morning break tomorrow, we'll make sure we get out there first, lock arms and stand tall. There's only one way in to our patch so he'll have to break us down or give up.' Bee has a habit of stealing other people's ideas and making them seem like hers. Luckily Copper Pie didn't care.

'Newboy's done for!' He made two fists and did a yob face. It wasn't much different from his regular face.

'Same,' said Fifty.

'Four against one. What's he gonna do?' said C.P.

I couldn't help thinking that he'd find some way round our plan. Newboy was definitely *not* your average kid.

the human
wall

Mum comes straight from work to pick up me and my sister, so although it's not very far, we go home in the car. I'd like to walk with Bee and Copper Pie but Mum says, 'I have to get Flo so I may as well take you too.' Fifty's not allowed to walk either.

Why don't mums get it? How are we meant to grow up and get a job and buy things on the internet and drive a car and shave and all the other things men do if we don't start practising basic skills like road-crossing now?

In the playground, Mum waits with Fifty's mum and his baby sister, Probably Rose. (They couldn't decide what to call her, so when anyone asked her name they said, 'Probably Rose', and it stuck.) Our two mums convince each other that they're bringing us up with the right amount of independence

– none. They're a bad combination: a doctor (my mum) and a pay-me-and-I'll-make-your-life-better therapist (that's what Fifty's mum is). When she asks you a question she stares into your eyes – it makes you blink and it's impossible to lie.

'How was your day, darling?' Mum asked.

Always the same question. Always answered by Flo before I have a chance. Even if I manage to start my first word before she does, she says her words anyway and mine get pulped.

'Mummy, Mr Dukes says we need a packed lunch and a raincoat.'

'Is that for your trip, darling?'

'Yes. It's not the day after, it's the day after the day after.' Flo has a problem with *tomorrow*. 'And we need five pounds for the shop.' She also lies.

The conversation went on and I thought about Newboy. I wondered whether we should have been a bit nicer to him the first time he came over. Then he'd have realised we weren't cool and moved on to some other kids instead and we wouldn't have to do the human barricade. It was worrying me already and it wasn't even tomorrow yet.

At home, Flo and I had toasted buns and apple juice and then I went up to my room. I took off my school sweatshirt, hung it over my desk chair, washed my hands and then settled down in my favourite place – my hammock (which hangs across the corner of my room next to my bookcase) – to finish *Stig of the Dump*. Reading took my mind off the head-to-head planned for morning break. If we weren't such good friends, I'd have been working out how to avoid it altogether. But it wasn't an option. Buddies are buddies.

KEENER'S FACT FILE

- Likes reading, building models
- Likes ALL computer games
- Is good at ALL computer games
- Brilliant skimboarder

- Doesn't like sticky things
- Doesn't like surprises
- Doesn't like sloppy food
- Doesn't like hair cuts (true surfboy)

FAMILY STUFF
Mum – doctor
Dad – something boring with a briefcase!?!
Sisters – Flo (small and bad) and Amy (big
          and bad)

It happened just before Flo woke me up. I was in a dream, and so was Newboy, except he was huge and wearing a yellow waistcoat and a bow tie (yes, seriously weird). He was heading straight for me with his extra-large boots and every time they hit the ground, the earth trembled. I wanted to run away but I was stuck to the ground with the strongest glue ever. I couldn't escape. Newboy grabbed me with a hand that was so big it went right round my middle and tried to pull me up but the glue was stronger than he was so my feet shot out of my purple (?!) shoes. He swung me round and round and threw me like a shot-put and I went flying. Suddenly I was on the ground . . . and there was blood. (I don't do blood. I am officially a wuss when it comes to pain.) He was standing over me about to finish me off when . . .

I felt Flo burrow into my bed for the daily cuddle. She thinks I like it but it's more that I'm so asleep I can't make my mouth say the words I need to say to get rid of her. By the time I'm on full power, she's gone to annoy Amy, my big sister. (Caution: avoid at all costs.)

Mum noticed my mood at breakfast. The worry had grown larger overnight.

'Is there something up?'

'No, I'm fine.' I did a fake smile and she carried on buttering the toast. Fifty's mum is much harder to convince. Her questions are the sort you can't answer yes or no to. Questions that start with 'how' and have the word 'feeling' in the middle.

In English first thing, Bee had another go at Newboy.

'Please, Miss Walsh. Can you ask him to stop rocking on the back legs of his chair? I keep thinking he's going to fall.'

Good one, Bee. It's Miss Walsh's pet hate. You get a warning the first time. Second time: straight detention. No question. Miss Walsh looked up from her desk. Newboy was sitting perfectly still on all four legs, like he had been all morning.

'Jonno, chairs are made with four legs for a reason,' she said, far too nicely. She was still being soft on him.

(*Jonno – what sort of name is that?* I thought.)

I didn't dare look at him. I looked at Copper Pie instead. He was leaning back on two legs, almost overbalancing, with a grin so wide it squashed his freckles together. I saw Fifty do a quick thumbs up.

But me, I was getting a bad feeling about it all. I kept my head down until break, trying to finish my story about an incredibly powerful sea creature wrecking all the fishing boats and poisoning the waters with its toxic waste.

We'd agreed to sprint straight outside to our territory as soon as the bell went. I was there second, behind Copper Pie. No one ever gets anywhere before him unless he's not going that way. He's the fastest in the school.

Between panting, I tried to abort the mission. 'How about we let him hang out with us for a bit? He'll soon see we're no fun.'

'Keener!' Copper Pie gave me the look he's used many times before. I'm *always* the one trying to stop the others from doing risky things. Most of the time Fifty feels the same but he relies on me to be the wimp. That's how it works in groups. You all have a job, like leader, ideas person, dangerman, Mr Responsible (that's me), funny one . . . Fifty's job is smooth talker. Bee is boss. Copper Pie is secret weapon.

'Take your positions,' Copper Pie shouted. He stood bang in the middle of the way in, with the wire fence of the netball court one side and the trees the other. I went to the right, blocking the gap that side. Fifty and Bee took care of the rest. We fidgeted a bit to get a tight fit and linked arms. Wedged into the space, we waited. I kept swallowing something that wasn't there.

I glanced behind at the tiny triangle of land with the rotten tree stump that we call our patch. It's always dark and often damp and even more often smelly. *Why did it matter so much?* I asked myself.

'He's coming,' said Bee.

'Time, my noble friends, to defend our homeland from the wretched Gauls,' said Fifty.

'Someone will lock you up one day, freak,' said C.P.

Fifty lives half in the real world and half in some other made-up universe but at least he'd answered my question: it mattered because to us it was a kind of home.

We all grew a bit taller as the enemy drew nearer. I stuck my chest out, but it made the butterflies in my stomach seem worse, so I tucked it in again.

What do you think Newboy did?

Ran at us like a snorting bull? No.

Karate-chopped our arms to break up the line? No.

Walked off? That would have been ideal but . . . No.

He strolled up to us with his hands in his pockets, a half-smile on his face, his glasses slightly too low down his nose so he looked like a professor.

'Is it the beginning of a dance? he said, making a puzzled crease down the middle of his forehead. 'Do you join arms and waltz round the playground?'

Nobody tells Copper Pie he's doing the waltz. Before any of us had a chance to think of a clever reply (not that I can *ever* think of one until I'm in the bath three days later), Copper Pie's arm disengaged from Fifty's, shot out and wrapped itself round Jonno's neck forcing his head down, ready for —

Sheesh! I had to do something.

Copper Pie tried to free his other arm – the hand was already shaped into a fist – but I held it firmly, squeezed between my elbow and my body. Getting another kid in a headlock was one thing but a full-blown assault was a whole lot worse. Copper Pie tried to shake me off but I wasn't going to let go. He'd have to punch me first. (That would NEVER happen. He's been my protector since nursery when Annabel Ellis used to bite me.) I held on long enough for Fifty and Bee to peel his other arm from around Jonno's neck and for Bee to whisper the magic word 'detention', followed by the other magic word 'suspension'. Copper Pie doesn't need any more trouble. He let Newboy go.

Jonno Joins

You've got to respect Jonno: he didn't hit Copper Pie, he didn't say something mean, he didn't cry or even do the wobbly bottom lip. I don't think he did anyway. I didn't look too closely – I was too ashamed. But not ashamed enough to actually help. Help came quickly enough from another direction.

'Are you all right? It's Jonno, isn't it?' Miss Maggs, the playground monitor, was by his side in a flash. Any hopes the attack hadn't been witnessed vanished. I let Copper Pie have his arm back and watched him head for the back entrance, because we all knew what was coming next.

Miss Maggs shouted after him, 'Wait outside the Head's office.'

Bee rolled her eyes. 'Another fine mess. Copper Pie will end up Prisoner Pie if he carries on like this.'

She's right. The last thing Copper Pie needs is another roasting from the Head. Why did Newboy have to get in the way?

Copper Pie
cops it

The thing about Copper Pie is that he's the best friend you could ever have in some ways, and a total disaster in others. He'll always stand up for you, lend you money, borrow money to lend you, eat your unwanted lunch, lie for you *and* would even lend you his brother, Charlie, to torture – not that anyone wants to. The trouble comes when someone annoys him. He doesn't seem to understand that other people think differently. No, that's not it. He doesn't understand that other people are *allowed* to think something different. But he *is* getting better . . . slowly.

The three of us discussed what we thought his punishment would be. He's had an essay on 'Using words to resolve issues' – I did that for him. And loads of lunchtime detentions for: being rough, unsportsmanlike behaviour (he kicked his

COPPER PIE'S FACT FILE

- Bright ginger hair
- Very freckly
- Awful at anything to do with dividing, timesing, spelling or school
- Good at everything sporty
- Loves football and food
- Likes war and weapons
- Very loyal

FAMILY STUFF

Mum – runs a nursery

Dad – lazy, according to his mum

Brother – Charlie, aged 3, snotty, stinky, sticky, stupid, absolutely not allowed in Copper Pie's room

goalie for letting in a pathetic shot), not sitting still in class (he was jumping on his desk because it wouldn't shut) and bringing a weapon to school (a catapult isn't really a weapon, is it? It's practical exploration of the basic mechanism of the Roman ballista).

Bee said, 'This time it'll be exclusion. A Year 6 getting a new kid in a headlock for no reason. Exclusion, for definite.'

'It was hardly no reason. He accused us of waltzing.' I sounded ridiculous. Bee started jogging on the spot (none of us know how to waltz) and giggling, and then me and Fifty joined in (the laughing, *not* the dancing).

I was last in the line-up for lunch, and still chuckling, when Jonno came along with an ice pack pressed against his neck. I shut up and turned to study the back of Bee's head, praying he wouldn't speak to me, or worse, punch me.

He didn't.

Copper Pie's punishments were: a talking to from the Head and Miss Walsh, an apology to Jonno, to stay in every lunch break this week and, worst of all, a letter home.

'It could have been worse,' said Bee.

'Could it? Mum's gonna hit the roof.' Even Copper Pie's freckles looked pale. His mum *is* quite shouty.

'You could have been suspended.' Bee shook her head and tutted.

We were eating slowly for a change, so that Copper Pie had less time sitting outside the Head's office on the naughty chair. I had plain pasta (no sauce), cheese, sweetcorn and a muffin: one of my favourite lunches.

'At least your mum won't start wailing, "Where did I go wrong?" like mine does and suggest we schedule in more "quality time",' said Fifty.

'Your mum's nice – well, apart from all the kissing,' said Bee. 'All my mum does is feed me and buy my school shoes. At least your mum's interested in you.'

'Too interested,' said Fifty. 'Kids aren't meant to be

interesting to their mothers. Kids like junk food and danger, that's it. Like C.P. here.'

For the first time since 'the incident' Copper Pie smiled. 'Don't forget telly and football.'

Fifty smacked him on the shoulder, which meant something like, 'You're our mate no matter what.'

Eventually we had to go out. Copper Pie went to meditate outside the Head's office and the three of us headed for the tree. I had a quick peek to make sure HE wasn't there. No. No sign of him. I didn't want to see Newboy for a while. I was worried he might have fingerprints on his neck.

Tuesday afternoons are my favourite. I got top marks in the science test so Miss Walsh put my name on the board in the tick column, making me officially a keener. Copper Pie was already up there with the crosses! And I worked hard at my model in D.T. – it's a Spitfire, made from two boxes and the cardboard tube from the kitchen roll all covered in brown paper with wooden sticks attaching the wheels, clear plastic for the windscreen and a working propeller with a battery under the wing. I can't wait to paint it. I've got a picture to copy so it'll be an exact replica. Fifty's making a fire engine. It's rubbish. He says he's going to burn it in the metal bin in his room.

The bell went and I still wasn't packed up so everyone skedaddled without me. When I came out, the playground was nearly empty. Fifty was waiting with my mum, my sister Flo, and (*what was HE doing there?*) Jonno. Peculiar. Unbelievably, after all that had happened, he was *still* bothering us. And where was *his* mum? She was obviously super-late.

As I walked towards them, Fifty stepped towards me doing a mini version of the cut-throat sign. He looked worried. Perhaps his mum was in with the Head who was advising her that her son should stop mixing with a certain ginger-haired ruffian. Perhaps my mum would be called in next?

'Disaster,' Fifty said in my ear. There was no time to ask what he meant because Mum was right behind him.

'There you are. Honestly, anyone would think you didn't want to come home.'

I smiled, keeping my eyes focused on Mum and not on Fifty who was making an I'm-being-strangled face behind her.

'It looks as though we've got a houseful for tea today. Come on, you lot.'

I started to walk beside Fifty – he was obviously coming for tea. He comes most weeks so it wasn't really a reason to make I'm-about-to-die faces, but he does like acting.

Mum and Flo followed . . . and so did Jonno.

He was probably hoping to be invited too, I thought. *No chance!*

I was about to ask Fifty what he thought Jonno the shadow was doing when Mum bent her head forward and whispered, 'It seemed kind to offer to have him round for tea. You don't mind, do you?'

What did she mean? Why did we need to be kind to Fifty? Why would I mind my friend coming over?

Uh-oh . . . A nasty thought found its way to the front of the queue.

Surely she couldn't mean Jonno?

No. Of course she couldn't. It wasn't possible that Jonno could be coming for tea because I hadn't mentioned a new boy to Mum. Maybe Fifty's mum was ill . . . or worse, in hospital. Yes, that would be it. Be kind to Fifty while we break the news. The fact that we were all walking together was a coincidence, that's all. Or maybe Jonno was still hoping to worm his way in with us, even though we'd shown him we weren't interested.

I couldn't wait to talk to Fifty about how *completely* crazy Newboy was.

Mum leaned forward again. 'Only I met Jonno's mum this morning at the surgery. It's so hard being the new boy in a class.'

tea with
the enemy

I didn't say anything. I couldn't. There was a tight feeling as though someone had bandaged up my lungs a bit too tight with parcel tape.

Loads of questions were flying around my head, out of my ears, back in through my nose, buzzing in front of my eyes.

Will Jonno rat on us?

If he does, what will Mum say?

If he doesn't, will we all pretend to get on like proper mates?

Will Jonno go along with it?

Will I be able to swallow my tea with Jonno staring at me?

Does Jonno have any telltale signs of being throttled?

The words started to reorganise themselves into nonsense:

I like to swallow throttled rat.

Mum drew level and gave me a worried look. 'I know you

don't like things that aren't planned, but Jonno's mum was so pleased that I asked, and when she suggested today . . .'

I could feel my legs start to tingle. Luckily Mum knows the signs.

'Take a breath NOW,' she ordered.

I did.

'That's right. And another.'

HOW I BECAME A BREATH-HOLDER

When I was a tiny baby and couldn't walk or talk or get food in my mouth without smearing it over my face first, my mum had a bright idea: I think I'll take this little baby (who can't even sit up) for a swim.

So she took me and my sister Amy (who was five) to the pool and (because she'd been told that babies can swim underwater) she let go of me. I floated below the water for a bit while she chatted to Amy and then (when she remembered I was there) she pulled me out of the water.

At that point, I was meant to take a big breath but no one had taught me that, so I didn't. That was the first time I went blue.

Amy says that after that I did it every time I didn't get my own way. But that's a lie.

Everything started to come back into focus. I've been a

breath-holder since before I could talk, although it doesn't happen very often now. I don't mean to do it. It just happens. I forget to breathe, go bluish and then faint. Luckily as soon as I begin to faint my body takes over and I start breathing again. Fifty's mum says it's attention-seeking behaviour. My mum says it's a quiet version of a tantrum and tells everyone to ignore me. That's what it's like having a mum-doctor! Even if I'm really ill, all I get given is a spoon of pink medicine and a vest.

The breathing helped. I needed to stay calm.

'The car's just along here. Jonno, would you like to sit in the front with me so we can get to know each other?'

'Thank you,' said Jonno. I hadn't noticed his voice before. It was proper, like on the radio.

Flo scrambled on to her seat and I got in the middle, followed by Fifty. Using faces and signs, we panicked silently. Mum did the talking. 'Your mum's description was spot on, Jonno. I had no trouble finding you.' She paused. 'So how are you settling in?'

'OK so far,' he said. *Phew!*

'Snack?' Mum asked as we walked into the house.

'Yes, please,' said Fifty and Jonno at the same time.

'Yes, please, Mummy,' said Flo. She's a creep.

The four of us sat at the kitchen table eating cheese biscuits and drinking blackcurrant. Luckily Flo chats to anyone so she made all the noise. I was completely mute. What could I say to a boy we'd deliberately told on for things he hadn't done, been rude to and practically beaten up?

'What are you going to do before tea?' Mum said.

Fifty could see I still wasn't functioning so he stepped in. 'I think we'll go outside and . . . find something to do there.'

'Good. What about you, Flo?'

'Can I do Play-Doh?'

'Of course,' Mum said. She cleared away the plates and sent us out.

So we stood on the grass.

My gaze was fixed on the wavy blades, the bright shiny green and the duller greyish green of the underside. I could easily have stopped breathing again. It would have been better than the embarrassment of not knowing what to say. And the worry that we'd *still* be standing in a silent circle when Mum called us for tea. And if she *never* called us for tea because a big wave swept her away, then we'd grow old and grey and die there. In between my desperate thoughts, a label kept gliding into view, like a subtitle on a film. It said, *SORRY*.

'Sorry,' said Fifty.

My head snapped up. 'Yes. Sorry.'

'Accepted,' said Jonno. 'I've had worse welcomes.'

Although we'd only said eight words between us, everything changed. Not speaking was so uncomfortable. Speaking was like finally having a pee when you've been holding on and holding on. Jonno grinned so I grinned back.

'Have you been to lots of schools?' asked Fifty.

'Enough. This is the fourth school in seven years.'

'Did you get expelled?' Fifty said.

'No, but I wouldn't have minded if I had. I've been to schools where the classroom is scarier than being in a cage with . . .' He paused.

'A panther?' I suggested.

'I was actually deciding between the devil and the tooth fairy, but a panther would do. Did you know there's no such species?'

'There is. It's black and it's a cat,' said Fifty.

'It's black and it's a cat, but it's actually a leopard or a jaguar with black skin. Opposite of an albino.'

'I didn't know that,' I said.

'Same,' said Fifty.

After that the questions flew: Why does he keep moving? When is he moving again? Why is he scared of the tooth fairy? (He isn't, any more.) Which school was the best? What is the worst thing that's happened to him? How far can he see without his glasses? (As far as his elbow.)

We started to chuck a ball around as we chatted and it was OK. (And his neck looked normal!) He'd lived in London and Glasgow, where he met his best friend, Ravi. His worst first day was in Oxford where the teacher asked a posh kid to show him the way to the loos and he showed him the girls' not the boys' and then went and got all the other boys so they could watch him come out. How nasty is that?

It was nice talking to someone new – we all know everything there is to know about each other.

Jonno asked questions too: Why do you have such strange nicknames? I can guess Keener, but Fifty? Copper Pie?

We enjoyed answering that.

NICKNAMES

COPPER PIE: Ages and ages ago (we must have been about six) he was eating in class (absolutely not allowed) and the fill-in teacher (a man who didn't know any of our names) shouted, 'You with the ginger hair, put down that sandwich.' And C.P. yelled back, 'My mum says it's copper, not ginger, and this is not a sandwich it's a pork pie.' He's been Copper Pie ever since.

FIFTY PER CENT (or FIFTY): He hasn't grown since he was about three, so he's half the size of everyone else.

BEE: Short for Beatrice.

KEENER: It's obvious, isn't it?

JONNO: Has never had a nickname.

'Do you want to go out the front?' I said. Our garden's quite small so we often play on the road.

We decided to play piggy in the middle, one on each side of the road and the pig in the middle, who had to try to get the ball *and* not get run down. I was in the middle, and had been for ages, when we heard yelling.

'Keener!' It was Copper Pie, and someone chasing him – Bee.

What were they doing here? My house isn't on the way to Bee's or C.P.'s. She lives on the estate and he lives on the main road.

Copper Pie skidded to a stop two drives down. So I ran over.

'What is it?'

'What's *he* doing here?' Copper Pie gave Jonno the evil eye.

'Long story. Mum invited him. He's all right.'

'He's the reason I'm for it.'

'Come on, Copper Pie. He just wanted someone to hang out with. Do you know he's never been at a school longer than about five minutes? He's *always* been the new boy.'

'So?'

'Anyway, why are you here?'

Bee caught up. 'Trouble. Big, big trouble.'

Fifty came over. 'Did I hear trouble is brewing, witchy-poo?'

'Brewed,' said Bee.

Copper Pie sat on the kerb and put his head in his hands.

Jonno Joins

Bee made an aren't-you-going-to-tell-them face, but he didn't look up.

'What is it?' I said. 'Did something happen on the way home?'

Bee shook her head.

'Well there wasn't time to get in any more trouble at school today,' I said. 'Was there?'

clumsy
clot

Bee did the talking.

'C.P. went back up to the classroom after D.T. to get his catapult. He thought he ought to leave it at home for a few days because of . . .' She stopped and stared at Jonno with big wide eyes that seemed to say, 'All your fault, Newboy.'

'Anyway, on the way back down the stairs he was just testing the elastic, he *says* . . .' (she made a ticking-off face at Copper Pie) 'when his finger slipped and . . .' (she winced) 'he knocked the left ear off the statue of Charles Stra-Stra-Stra-att-on . . .'

The last word got longer and longer because it was interrupted by little snorts as though she was trying not to cry.

I gasped. The statue stands in the corridor right outside

the hall doors. Charles Stratton was the founder of the school hundreds of years ago. I could see why she was upset. It's probably priceless.

Bee took a breath and finished her sentence without any gaps, '. . . withafiftypencepiece,' and then let out a huge 'HA HA HA', sat down on the pavement and carried on laughing her head off.

'I'm sorry, Copper Pie, but only you could be *so* stupid and *so* unlucky,' said Fifty, grinning away.

I couldn't see what was funny about damaging such a valuable part of the school's history but all the rest of them were in fits.

'You're right. I never hit anything I'm aiming at,' said Copper Pie, who seemed to find it just as hilarious as the others even though he was in terrible trouble.

'Listen,' I said.

No one did.

'Listen! This is serious.' I wondered if perhaps I wasn't making any noise because no one seemed to hear.

'Stop! It's not funny.'

Finally, they stopped.

'You're right, Keener. It's not at all funny. Poor Charles is deaf in one ear now,' said Fifty, before he started laughing again.

'I think it's more a case of amputation,' said Bee, wiping tears off her cheek. It's weird. She always cries when she laughs. Her tear ducts must be wired up wrong.

'Stereo to mono with one flick of elastic,' added Fifty.

'And nothing to rest his glasses on,' said Jonno, who had walked over.

There was a pause while we worked out the joke.

'Good one,' said Copper Pie.

You see, that's the other thing about Copper Pie: he's not complicated. I don't mean he's simple, as in thick, but he's straightforward.

Jonno wasn't wanted on our patch, so he told him to go away.

Jonno annoyed him, so he hit him.

Jonno said something clever, so he congratulated him.

I said Jonno was all right, so Copper Pie gave him a chance.

'So what are you going to do about it?' Jonno asked Copper Pie.

'I dunno. Hope no one notices.'

'Is it safe to do that?' Jonno went on. 'I mean . . . did anyone see you?'

'No one saw me hit it . . . but Walsh saw me going up the stairs. She was coming down.'

'What about when you left?'

'Miss Maggs was still in the playground.'

'Any other kids about?' Jonno was giving him the third degree.

'Only Bee. It was well late.'

'What were you doing all that time?' I asked.

Copper Pie didn't answer.

Bee sighed. 'We went to see if we could intercept the letter from the Head to Copper Pie's mum and dad.'

'What?' I shouted.

'It was just an idea,' said Bee. 'And we didn't find it anyway.'

'It's illegal you know, interfering with the Royal Mail,' I said.

'Never mind about that,' said Fifty. 'Damaging the statue's the problem. Punishment for that won't just be a letter. It'll be an invitation for C.P.'s whole family to sit outside the Head's office.'

'There aren't enough chairs,' said Bee.

'They could bring their own sofa,' said Fifty.

'This isn't helping,' said Copper Pie.

'What are the chances you'll get away with it?' asked Jonno.

Copper Pie screwed up his face. 'Not good.'

There was lots of nodding from the rest of us. C.P. gets blamed for most things whether he's done them or not.

'So the only way out of this that I can see is if we make sure no one notices the damage – that way they won't be looking for a culprit.' Jonno had a good way of putting things. 'Have you got the ear? Is it in one piece?'

'Yes and no. It's not what you'd call an ear any more.'

'Let's see.'

Copper Pie fished deep into his pockets and pulled out

37

some bits of grey stone tangled up with some string, three rubber bands and two empty crisp packets, both beef flavour.

'You really shouldn't eat those. They're in the top five of the junk food table.'

'Not now, Bee,' said Fifty.

The ear was like one of those frustrating puzzles you get at Christmas that start off as a nice shape but can never be put back together again.

KEENER'S WORST
CHRISTMAS STOCKING PRESENTS EVER

- A rubber dog toy
- Union Jack pants
- Slime (ear wax colour)
- Coal
- Squashed satsuma
- Pinocchio pencil sharpener

'Well, that's not going back on,' said Bee. 'And someone will definitely notice a missing ear. I mean, it's assembly tomorrow and we line up *right next* to Charles.'

Jonno shook his head. 'They might not. But it's going to take team work.'

'What is?' said Fifty.

'Fixing the statue of course.'

Jonno had gone from the unwanted member to the one

who had us all listening. *How did he do that?*

'Have you got a master plan?' said Fifty.

'I might have. Do you want to hear it?'

'Too right,' said Copper Pie. 'And, er . . . sorry about the headlock.'

'You've got scarily fast reactions,' said Jonno. 'I'm glad Keener held on to you because I didn't fancy the punch that was coming next.'

Jonno looked at me when he said that and did a sort of nod. It got me thinking that although I was trying to save Copper Pie from trouble, it was really Jonno that I'd helped. I don't do a lot of rescuing so I felt quite proud. I nodded back in what I hoped was an it's-no-big-deal-I-do-it-every-day way.

'Go on, then,' said Bee. 'Spit it out. How do we get Copper Pie off the hook?'

team
talk

'The first thing is we need to be a team,' said Jonno.

'You said that already,' said Bee. 'We're mates – of course we're a team.'

'Are you? Because I reckon if you'd been working more as a team you'd have had a better chance of getting rid of me. I mean, how good was your plan?'

Jonno looked at us, one at a time. I felt my face go red. I've got blond hair and pale skin that turns an unnatural raspberry colour when I feel embarrassed. Fifty started kicking a woodlouse with his shoe. Bee retied her ponytail. Copper Pie kept his head down.

Please someone say something.

No one did. Jonno carried on.

'Think about it. Copper Pie told me to go away, but no

one backed him up – unless Bee's personal bubble thing was meant to scare me off. Fifty had a go at me in class but Miss Walsh let me off. If you'd made up more lies about me, she'd have thought I was a troublemaker and that would have made things really difficult for me. Same when Bee did it. And when you finally barricaded the way in to your base, all of you working together, one of you broke ranks and ruined what was the best action you'd taken. I was hardly going to body slam the four of you just to sit in the dirt under your tree.'

He made us sound like a bunch of wallies.

'We're not used to having to defend ourselves,' I said, a bit cross at his know-all attitude.

'But he's got a point,' said Fifty. 'If it was footie and your team had a corner, you'd never score if everyone did their own thing. Every player needs to know what the others are going to do to stand a chance of getting a goal. That's what you're saying, isn't it, Jonno?'

'Pretty much. If you'd stuck together I'd have probably given up.'

Bee was getting impatient. 'OK. OK. We're a rubbish team. But what's the plan for the ear?'

He had us all waiting with our tongues hanging out. I really believed he was going to unveil a devilishly clever scheme, but instead he said, 'Simple. We replace it before registration tomorrow.'

'Great idea!' said Bee sarcastically. 'I wonder why *I* didn't think of that? We stick this mess back on and everything's OK. Happy ending.'

'Perhaps not that exact mess but basically, yes.'

I was getting pretty annoyed but strangely Fifty was smiling.

'Go on, tell us the magic ingredient in your plan, Merlin,' he said.

SPECIAL TALENTS

JONNO: Brainwashing people to make them do crazy things.

COPPER PIE: Eating masses of food very fast and not getting fat.

FIFTY: Hide and seek, fits into impossibly small spaces.

BEE: Picking her nose with her tongue AND winning 'guess the name of the doll' and 'how many sweets in the jar' at EVERY school fair.

KEENER: Remembering phone numbers and car registrations (would make good spy if bit braver).

Jonno shrugged. 'We make an ear shape out of something else. We cover the doors to make sure no one sees us stick it on.

It won't look great but the "magic", if there is any, is human nature. As long as the ear is roughly the same shape and colour as the old one, no one will notice because people see what they expect to see. Not what's really there. It's a fact.'

'Are you telling me that if we stick a cauliflower to the side of Charles Stratton's head no one will realise?' I said, expecting everyone to laugh.

No one did.

'As long as the cauliflower's roughly the right size and colour . . . yes.' Jonno's face was completely serious.

'You're mad,' I said.

'Rugby players have cauliflower ears. They get squashed in the scrum and their ears go bumpy,' said Copper Pie. We ignored him.

'Perhaps it's not mad,' said Fifty, who had been quite quiet. 'Have you ever heard your mum say to your dad, "Darling, do you notice anything different about me?"' He used a squeaky girly voice and ran his fingers through his curls. 'And your dad stands there with absolutely no idea what she's on about, and your mum spins round and your dad's sweating, knowing he hasn't got a clue, willing his eyes to spot what's improved or changed colour, or disappeared altogether, and he says, "New haircut? New dress? Facelift?"'

'And she shakes her head and looks annoyed and he tries even harder, "New earrings? No glasses?" (She doesn't even wear glasses.) "You've lost weight?"'

'And finally, before she slams the door in his face, she says,

"I've had the enormous hairy mole removed from my chin".'

'That's what happened when Dad grew his beard. Mum didn't notice for weeks,' said Copper Pie.

'So do you mean everyone will see our mashed-potato ear or whatever it is, but in their heads they'll see the old one?' said Bee.

'Almost. Although I think the point is that they won't even see the new ear,' said Jonno. 'If you see something everyday you don't really look at it at all, you just use the picture you have in your head from before.'

'Please revert to saved image,' said Fifty, in a robot voice.

'Cool,' said Copper Pie.

Amazing. They all believed him. Just like that. All we had to do was put a bit of cauliflower covered with grey mould on the founder's head and, according to Jonno, it had never happened.

I wasn't going to make a fuss but I had my doubts.

'OK. Best material for the ear. Any suggestions?' said Jonno.

Fifty: 'Dough.'

Me: 'Pastry.'

Bee: 'Blu-Tack.'

Me: 'I know, that foam that you fill cracks with.'

Copper Pie: 'Plasticine. Pitta bread.'

Fifty: 'Cardboard.'

Bee: 'Rice cakes.'

Fifty: 'Wet nappies – they look grey.'

Bee: 'A shell.'

Copper Pie: 'Bogies.'

Bee took over. 'Zip it. All of you.' We all did what she said. We usually do. 'I have no idea how to make an ear —'

'Nor me,' said Copper Pie.

Bee looked at me, Fifty and Jonno. 'So why don't you three make one while you're here at Keener's for tea?'

'Fine by me,' I said.

'Same,' said Fifty.

'Good. That means we can concentrate on working out how we get the thing stuck on without being seen,' said Bee.

'What time does school open?' asked Jonno.

Copper Pie looked at his watch. 'Oh no! I'm meant to be home. I've got to go.'

'A few minutes won't make any difference. And anyway, I'll come with you. Your mum never shouts when I'm there,' said Bee.

'Yes, she does.'

'Well, she might not today.'

'So when does school open?' I said. I'm never there till just before the bell.

'Quarter past eight,' said Copper Pie. He gets in early to avoid all the babies arriving at his house. His mum runs a nursery on the bottom floor and they do their living in the top two.

'OK,' said Jonno. 'Let's meet at eight-fifteen at the end of that alley near —'

'No. Not the alley,' we all said before he could finish.

'Make it the bus stop,' said Bee.

Jonno looked confused but changed the plan anyway. 'OK.'

'Agreed,' said Bee. 'But then what?'

'First thing is to make sure no one comes in while we're fixing Stratton's hearing aid, so how about this: we spill some water and then guard the doors and tell everyone who tries to come in, "The floor's slippery so go round the back, please".'

Not bad, but . . .

'What if a teacher comes along, or the Head?' I asked.

'They never do,' said Copper Pie. 'The back door's nearer the car park and they go straight up the back stairs to the staffroom to down double-strength coffee before they have to face us.'

'But what about the ones who come on the bus . . . or walk?' I asked.

'We could try and send them round the back,' said Bee. 'And if they insist on coming in we show them the water . . . I suppose.' She looked at Jonno – surely bossy Bee wasn't checking to see what he thought.

'That would work fine,' said Jonno. 'All their concentration will be on the wet floor, which will stop them looking at the statue. And if anyone's coming through, whoever's guarding the door can shout something like, "Don't slip, Miss," as a warning, so the ear surgeons have time to get away from Charlie Stratton before they're caught.'

'What if we're told off for playing with water?' said Fifty. 'Hey, do you remember that water tray we had in Reception with the sailing boats?'

'Grow up, Fifty,' said Bee. 'We can say we think it was the cleaners who did it.'

'Sounds good to me. All bases covered. I've got to go. Come on, Bee.' Copper Pie was up and ready to run.

'Hang on,' said Bee. 'Who's doing what?'

'I'm always there early so I'll guard the main door.' Copper Pie's suggestion got nods all round.

'Makes sense. People are used to seeing you hanging around,' Fifty said.

'And me?' said Bee.

'How many other ways are there to get to the statue?' Jonno asked.

'Well, the stairs, obviously,' she said. 'And the canteen, but no one goes there first thing, so it's really just if someone comes in the back door and doesn't head for the staff room. I can cover both.'

'Excellent,' said Jonno. 'Best to be prepared.'

'Looks like I'm water monitor then,' said Fifty.

'So we're on ear duty,' said Jonno, looking at me.

'Right. Off we go then.'

Copper Pie grabbed Bee's arm but before they could skedaddle Jonno said, 'Hey! Put it there,' and held his hand out. Copper Pie slapped his hand down on top – it made a thwack. Bee did the same.

'Come on, guys,' said Jonno.

My hand joined the tower, then Fifty's. Jonno moved his

hand up and down and counted, 'One, two, three', and then pushed all our hands up really hard so they flew high in the air.

'See you tomorrow,' we all said.

Tea was ready.

'Have you got a best friend?' asked Flo.

'Yes, but he lives miles away in Scotland,' said Jonno.

'What's his name?'

'He's called Ravi.'

'That's the name for pasta,' she said.

'That's rude, Flo,' I said.

She ignored me.

'Have you got a sister? asked Flo.

'No. There's only me,' Jonno answered. 'I'd like one though.'

'Trust me, you wouldn't,' I said.

'Don't be mean, Keener,' said Fifty. 'Flo's an excellent sister. Look, she can make Play-Doh pigs.' He pointed at the little models she'd arranged round her plate.

'They're not pigs, they're babies,' she said. 'Muuuum! Fifty said my babies are . . .'

We bolted our food and escaped to get on with ear creation in my room.

I put away all my special models whenever someone comes round because I'd rather no one touched them, but because I hadn't had any advance warning, they were all laid out on the floor in their special positions. I've got a whole army of vehicles with different weapons. We had to tiptoe carefully between them. Jonno was really interested. They're all either Lego or made from junk. I showed him where the Spitfire is going to sit when it's ready. He picked up my Deathmobile. I didn't want him to but he was really careful so I forgot to be bothered and explained how the missiles fly out from underneath instead. He had a go at shooting Fifty, who was swinging in my hammock, but he hit my skimboard by mistake.

'Cool board,' Jonno said. 'Can you surf?'

'I can, but I like skimming better.'

He'd never heard of it, so I said we'd take him with us next time my dad and I had a boy's trip to Devon.

Eventually Fifty reminded us we were meant to be ear making.

'Right. What shall we use?' I said.

We started another long list of rubbish suggestions: cotton wool, tofu, mushrooms, buy a joke ear . . .

'STOP!' shouted Fifty. 'We're getting nowhere. How about we each have a go on our own and see which one's best?'

'Fine by me,' I said.

'OK,' said Jonno.

We decided to bring our three ears into school and let the group pick the winner. I was quite looking forward to a bit of sculpture.

The doorbell rang. Mum shouted up to us, Jonno ran down, shouted 'Bye' and was gone.

'I'm glad he went first,' I said.

'Why? He's OK I think,' said Fifty.

'It's not him. I just don't know how I'm going to get to school by quarter past eight. Mum always drops me off.'

'We could walk together.'

'Will your mum let you?'

He chewed his lip. 'Well . . . she will if our class are having a walk-to-school day.'

'But we're not.'

'Looks like we are now,' he said.

I'm not keen on lying to Mum but this was an emergency. If I was going to be in on the ear surgery, I couldn't go in the car with Mum and Flo.

'Can you say it to my mum before you go?' I asked. 'She likes you.'

'I'll say it when mine comes to get me. Sort it out with both of them at the same time.'

You see, if I'm the wimp in the group, Fifty is the quick thinker and people handler. He knows the right thing to say and the way to say it.

Both our mums were pleased to hear about the walk-to-school campaign, but a bit surprised we hadn't mentioned it before. I decided not to think about the possibility of Mum mentioning it to any other parents, or to Miss Walsh.

'So I'll drop him off at eight as they seem to want to make the most of the early morning!' Fifty's mum said as she left.

FIFTY SAYING GOODNIGHT
TO HIS LITTLE SISTER

Fifty: Who's my lovely lickle ickle sister?

Probably Rose: Ba.

Fifty: Did you like your bath?

Probably Rose: Ba.

Fifty: Shall I tell you what your big brother's been doing?

Probably Rose: Ba.

Fifty: I've been making an ear.

Probably Rose: Ba.

Fifty: You know Copper Pie? The one with the red hair who always turns you upside down and says you like it?

Probably Rose: Ba ba.

Fifty: He broke the school statue but we're going to mend it.

Probably Rose: Ba.

Fifty: Are you going to bye byes now you've had your milky-milk?

Probably Rose: Yog-ert.

Fifty: Did you say yoghurt?

Probably Rose: Yog-ert.

Fifty: MUM! Probably Rose can speak! Probably Rose can speak!

operation:
save Copper Pie

Fifty wanted to see mine on the way to school but I wouldn't let him.

'I bet you haven't even made one.'

'I have, I'm just not showing it.'

'Keener, come on.'

'No. No. No.'

He gave up . . . eventually, and started on his favourite subject.

'Guess what?' he said.

'Guesswhats' are always something to do with his little sister. He's mad about her. I've told him, 'They start off cute and end up like Flo – poison,' but he doesn't believe me. I get daily reports on eating lumps without choking, turning over, clapping . . . and other startlingly brilliant achievements.

'Hang on, I'm thinking,' I said. 'Don't tell me – Probably Rose has learned to tie her shoelaces?'

'Don't be stupid.'

'Mastered chess?'

His bottom lip was sticking out – he doesn't like being teased about Rose.

'Go on then,' I said. 'What's she done now?'

'She can speak.' His big blue eyes were all excited and his curly hair was bouncing up and down.

Yeah, right!

'Fifty, she says "ba" all the time. That's not speaking – that's noise.'

'No, really. She said "Yoghurt".'

'No way.'

We talked about Jonno after that – it was a safer subject. (Safer than the sparks Fifty was making with the firesteel that he's not meant to bring to school! Actually, he'd make a good firesteel salesman: *Start a fire, anywhere. A slow firm strike against the steel produces a spark of up to 3000°C.*)

'Shall we let him come on our patch now?' Fifty asked me.

'Could do. Depends on the others.' I tried to sound not bothered but inside I was hoping Jonno could be one of us. We have loads of conversations that start with, 'What shall we do?' That wouldn't happen with Jonno.

The other three were already at the bus stop.

'At last. The bus drivers keep stopping to let us on and we have to wave them past,' said Bee. 'Let's go.'

We stopped at the bench inside the school gates.

'Right, it's ear-picking time,' said Fifty.

'I hate ear-pickers,' said Bee. 'The yellow stuff is *so* smelly.'

'Says the girl who can pick her nose with her tongue,' said Fifty.

'But I choose not to.'

'Come on, ears out,' said Copper Pie.

Secretly I was sure mine would win. I'd cut up a grey cardboard egg box that had a rough crumbly look to it, similar to the bits of ear from Copper Pie's pocket that I'd kept for reference. Using my glue gun, I'd stuck on a lobe at the bottom, a flap at the top and a rim all the way round. I'd even made a fold so the ear could be glued on easily.

'Ta da,' said Fifty as he pulled out a plasticine ear. And then, 'Oh!' as he realised the turquoise was showing through where the grey paint had flaked off.

That was his chance gone. I thought I'd wait till last for maximum glory but Jonno seemed to be doing the same.

'Come on,' said Bee.

I brought out my box, slowly opened the lid and displayed my perfect ear. I got a clap from Bee. 'It's wicked.' My thoughts exactly.

Jonno reached into his trouser pocket and out came a grey rubber ear. 'I cut it off my elephant.'

'No way,' said Copper Pie. 'That's sick. You severed his ear!'

C.P. likes elephants (particularly Trumpet, his cuddly toy!).

'It's not sick. It's genius. Look.' Fifty snatched it and held it up by his head. It did actually look quite human-ear-ish in a big lobe way.

'OK. Time to vote and get sticking. One vote each.'

Copper Pie voted for me, and so did I. Fifty voted for Jonno and so did Bee (traitors). That just left Jonno.

'I'll go for Keener's.'

I win. I win! It was brilliant . . . for about a second, but then I realised that I'd only really won because I voted for myself. Jonno must have thought his was best so he was just being nice, or creeping, by voting for mine.

'Actually, I vote for Jonno's.'

'Too late. We're going with egg-box-ear,' said Jonno.

'Positions, everyone,' said Copper Pie, as we walked to the double doors of the school entrance. You can tell he's football captain (although he nearly wasn't after the kicking-the-goalie episode).

Bee sat on the bottom step of the staircase. 'I've got a view of both the other entrances from here.'

Fifty went to get the water. Jonno and I went over to Charles Stratton. His head and shoulders sit on a special wooden platform, a bit like what posh people have in their hallways for plants. Jonno pulled out a piece of sandpaper, reached up and smoothed the skin in preparation for the transplant (he'd thought of everything). I got out the ear, put my all-purpose extra strong glue on the folded piece and when, at the last minute, my hands started to shake, Jonno took over and pressed the ear in place.

I stepped back to have a good look. It was weird. If you stared at the ear it was clearly wrong, but if you stared at his huge conk, or at his curled up lips or his concrete hair, the ear just blended in.

Fifty came back saying, 'I haven't got anything to put the water . . .', then started whooping when he saw the ear. Copper Pie must have heard because he abandoned his post.

'Not bad.' He had a closer look. 'Not bad at all.'

'Go egg-box-ear!' said Bee.

'Best example of glue ear I've ever treated,' said Jonno. (Fifty didn't get it so I told him glue ear is what little kids get. Snot in the ears basically.)

No need for the doormen or the cover story. The job was done. Time for a quick exit.

'Let's scram before anyone . . .' said Jonno.

We legged it to the trees, slipstreaming Copper Pie as usual.

'Put it here,' said Jonno and we did the piling-on-hands-thing again. This time with strange noises: *Yeowww*, *Yesssirree*, and *Way-to-go*.

Everyone was a bit over-excited. I looked round at my friends. It felt good. All we had to do was get to assembly without anyone raising the alarm.

'Make sure you don't keep looking at it or other people will too,' whispered Jonno a bit later, as we went down the stairs. 'Pass it on.'

As I said it to Fifty, a sick feeling started to replace the nice one.

What if I hadn't put enough glue on and it had fallen off already?

What if someone knocked it?

What if Jonno was wrong and everyone spotted the fake ear and started pointing and laughing?

What if . . .

I heard the word 'breathe'. It was Fifty. I breathed.

As we turned the corner to line up outside the hall, I kept my eyes well away from Charles Stratton. And well away from the others. So far so good.

There was the usual shoving as we took our place along the wall, and some talking, which isn't allowed.

'Quiet now,' said Miss Walsh as she swung round the corner with Callum carrying her stuff – he's a complete creep. And the most-hated boy in our class. And the best sportsman, after Copper Pie.

I looked at her. *Would she notice?*

She looked up at the clock above the hall doors.

'While we wait for the Head and the other classes, let's think about what the school would have been like three hundred years ago when Charles Stratton set it up.' She waved her hand across his face.

All eyes were on the head and shoulders of our founder. Except mine, because I couldn't look.

I waited for the first shouts of, 'Miss, his ear's not right,' or worse, 'Miss, he's got an egg carton not an ear and it looks like Keener made it.'

None came. There were thirty kids staring at his face and not one of them seemed to realise he had an egg-box-ear. My panic gave way to an overwhelming urge to laugh. *Idiots.*

I felt a pinch and turned to see Bee purple in the face and blown up like a balloon. She obviously didn't dare open her mouth. I quickly looked away but there weren't many safe places to look. Copper Pie was bent over making little squeaky sounds. Jonno was staring at the ceiling, which I assumed was his way of not losing his cool. Fifty had his hand over his eyes but his shoulders were going up and down so I assume he was doing one of those silent deep-inside laughs that make you cry.

Please let the Head come very very soon. Other kids were starting to notice the five weird children: shady eyes, bent over, stargazer, blueberry face and me, flibbertigibbet. (I like that word. I think it means silly but it sounds like it means someone who flits between lots of things, which is what my eyes were doing.)

The door creaked. At last, the other classes. And the Head.

Miss Walsh opened the hall door and our class began to troop in, followed by the others. Unbelievably no one, not one person, spotted the false ear.

Assembly was dull (not that I'd have been able to concentrate if it was interesting. It was too fantastic that we'd fooled

EVERYONE). It was all about Earth Day. Evidently it's our generation that will have to save the planet. *Fat chance*. When the Head had finished her sermon, Jonno put up his hand and asked to be excused. *Strange*. People can usually hold on long enough to last through assembly. Must have been the excitement of the early morning adventure. He got back just as we started filing out.

I risked one last look at Charles. Did I have a shock? It was almost me who blew it by shouting and pointing. The egg-box-ear was gone! A rubber elephant ear was in its place. I searched out Jonno with my eyes. He winked. I winked back. I knew why he'd done it. It wasn't because he wanted us to use his ear. He wanted to show that even a cauliflower floret would have worked. I couldn't wait for break to see if the others had noticed.

'Bee!'

Oh no! Why was the Head shouting at Bee? I looked round to see if it was a mistake. Maybe there was a real bee buzzing about.

'Could you wait there with, er . . . let me see . . .' The Head saw me staring. 'Keener. Yes, you.'

No. Not me. I can't lie to the Head. How does she know it was us?

I wished I'd excused myself like Jonno and stayed in the loo till break.

Bee and I watched everyone else disappear. The Head was chatting to Mr Morris so we did as we were told and waited, right by the statue. My heart was pumping at double time making my face go red and my armpits soggy. I wanted to tell on Copper Pie, explain about the catapult, but knew I couldn't. Me and Bee would have to take the blame.

HOW WE GOT THE TEACHERS TO USE OUR NICKNAMES

Miss Walsh is newish. On her first day she asked us all to tell her a bit about ourselves including our proper names and what we like to be called. She meant, if you're Michael, would you rather be Mike? When it was C.P.'s turn he said, 'I'm George but I'd like you to call me Copper Pie.

She thought it was a joke and giggled, but Bee said (in a very serious voice), 'Miss, why are you teasing our friend?' C.P. lifted up the lid, put his head in his desk and pretended to be very upset. (He was actually trying not to laugh out loud.) Miss Walsh didn't know what to do and he wouldn't bring his head out so in the end she agreed to call him Copper Pie.

Then it was Fifty's turn. 'My name is Thomas but I'm known as Fifty.' He lifted the lid of his desk up a weeny bit so she quickly said, 'Fine.' All I had to do was follow the others. (I'm not telling you what my other name is because it's ridiculous.) After a while the Head started using our 'chosen names' (that's what she calls them) too. She probably can't remember our real ones.

Mr Morris ran up the stairs and we were left with the Head.

'Right, Bee. Do you have anything you'd like to tell me?'

Bee pushed her fringe out of her eyes and opened her mouth, but nothing came out.

'Shall I give you a hint?'

Bee did a big swallow that made her neck look like a turkey's and said, 'Yes, please.'

'Let's see . . . It's most often grey, we use it all the time . . .'

Bee looked frozen with terror. So the Head stopped and turned on me.

'Perhaps Keener could help?'

My turn to be quizzed. Would I crack under pressure?

'I'm not sure.'

'Why do you think I've picked on Bee *this* day of all days? Earth Day.'

'Because we've given the statue a new ear,' didn't seem to be the answer. Nor was, 'Because you shouldn't dismember elephants on Earth Day?' likely to be what she was looking for.

'Because she's . . .' My mouth was ahead of my brain. I had no idea what to say. And then all of a sudden I did . . .

'Because she's into environmental things. Because she's made a recycling box in our classroom for all the cardboard we bring in our packed lunches. Because it's the sort of thing Earth Day's all about.'

Yippee! Not about the ear.

'Well done, Keener. On the ball as usual. Bee, Miss Walsh told me about your initiative and it occurred to me you would be an excellent person to champion a *Go Green* project within the school. Have a look at the Earth Day website and come and talk to me next week. Keener can be your second-in-command.'

'Thank you very much,' I said.

'Great!' said Bee. 'Really great!'

When we got to the patch, Bee had the others in stitches explaining how she thought the Head was on about the ear. Good job we didn't confess.

There was even more laughing about Jonno's substitution, which they'd all spotted.

'We should do it to other things,' said Copper Pie. 'Add beards to the paintings in the hall.'

'Change the teachers' names on the classroom doors,' said Bee.

'It doesn't have to be bad stuff. We could make up challenges,' I said.

'Same,' said Fifty. 'Getting Copper Pie out of trouble is fine, but we don't need to start making problems for ourselves.'

'I know, we could make things better . . . sort out all the litter in the playground . . . do something for charity . . . stop Callum's lot barging into the little ones' games. If we work together, we could *really* change things,' said Bee. Her eyes were all shiny and mad-looking.

'Yeah. We could be a proper gang with weapons . . . and tattoos,' said Copper Pie.

I rolled my eyes at exactly the same time as Fifty. I was on the downward roll when I noticed Jonno was rolling his too. *Great minds think alike!*

'And code words and rules and a motto,' I said.

'We could all have jobs,' Fifty said. 'Let's work out who can do what.'

Everyone started shouting out what they were good at and what the rest of us were bad at. Most of it was stupid.

	BEST AT:	WORST AT:
C. P.:	Running very fast	Red hair jokes
FIFTY:	Making fires	Putting out fires
KEENER:	Being teacher's pet	Wrestling
BEE:	Being bossy	Being bossed
JONNO:	Statue repair	Marmite

Bee said, 'As I'm the bossy one, I say let's work out who does what when the gang's properly sorted out.'

'I don't want us to be a gang,' said Jonno.

What did he mean? Of course we should be a gang.

It's brilliant. We could have a ceremony and swear to die for each other . . . press our bloody thumbs together and pledge our allegiance. (Not with real blood though, urghh!)

'Why not?' said Copper Pie.

'People don't like gangs. They're evil.'

'How about a club?' I said.

'Geek,' said Bee. 'Clubs are for chess.'

'Got it,' said Jonno. 'Why don't we form a tribe? Tribes are more serious, more loyal and they have rituals and if you've joined you can never leave. It would be special wouldn't it? A tribe.'

'You mean bongo drums and sacrifices?' said Copper Pie. Trust him.

Jonno gave him a funny look but didn't say anything, so I did. 'A tribe doesn't mean witch doctors and spears. A tribe is a name for a group of people who respect each other and share the same way of life and live in peace alongside other tribes.' There were trust-Keener-to-know looks all round. 'In lots of tribes everyone is equal. There's a chief but he doesn't sit around doing nothing and have servants. He does the same as everyone else. And tribes have a strong idea of what makes them different from everyone not in their tribe. That's good too. We've always been different, haven't we?'

'You mean because we've never bothered with the rest of the class?' said Fifty.

'Yes. And loyalty is a really important part of being in a

tribe and we're definitely loyal or we wouldn't have mended Charles Stratton, would we?'

'Tribe,' said Fifty as though he was trying it out. 'OK. I'm for it.'

'Copper Pie?' said Jonno.

'If it means you're gonna get me out of the poo every time, yep, I'm in.'

'Bee?'

'I'm not sure I get it but I definitely don't want to be left out . . . so yes. In. But I'm not wearing a grass skirt.'

I couldn't wait for Jonno to ask me. I wasn't going to be Keener any more – the quiet hard-working boy with the floppy blond hair who's never ever had a detention. I was going to be Keener of Tribe. It felt like my life was starting. In one day everything had changed. I knew I was part of something amazing. I just knew.

'Count me in,' I said in a big bold voice, twice as loud as normal. You see, it was starting already.

Alley
Cats

a bit
of bother

I didn't expect to have anything to report so quickly, but finding a second problem to sort out didn't take any time at all. The day after we formed Tribe, in the tiny gap between leaving school and getting to mine for the first Tribe pow-wow, Copper Pie and Jonno managed to run into trouble.

There were loads of important things to decide at the meeting like: a den outside school, code words for when non-Tribers were listening and a manifesto (Bee's grand idea – I think it's something to do with having an important purpose, like saving the planet, that you write down and keep as a reminder). I'd thought of more things too: a time capsule (we could put my notebook about Tribe in it together with other stuff about us – like fact files and photos), a magazine, and maybe even a promise we all have to say, like at Scouts.

Bee arrived at six o'clock, as agreed. I asked Amy (my fifteen-year-old sister) to send the others up to my room when they came.

'It will be a pleasure, little bro,' she said. 'Especially if you stay there.'

Mum had a late surgery. She does every Thursday. Amy walks me and Flo home. I like Thursdays because Amy and Flo always have girly time – painting nails or hair plaiting – and I get to do what I want with no interruptions.

'Don't do anything I wouldn't do,' she shouted as we disappeared upstairs.

'What's your sister done to her face?' asked Bee.

I shrugged.

'Well, something's different.'

'She's got a boyfriend.'

'Mank. That must be it. Snogging. I'm never doing that.'

'Nor me.'

Copper Pie and Fifty arrived together at 6:07 p.m.

'Where do you think Jonno is?' I asked.

'Got lost maybe,' said Fifty.

'He's been here before.'

'Maybe he dropped his glasses down a drain and is trying to hook —'

Bee cut Fifty off. 'Copper Pie, has your mum had the letter from school yet? The one about strangling Jonno.'

'Came this morning. Postman gave it to me, luckily.'

'Why is that lucky?' said Fifty.

I knew the answer before it came. Copper Pie had pocketed it. Normally I'd worry about something like that but I just wanted to get on. Ideas were queuing up in my head, waiting to be let out: we could keep a register, get matching T-shirts made, have membership cards . . .

'Maybe we should ring Jonno?' I said.

'Stop clucking, Keener. He's only . . . twelve minutes late. Take a chill pill.'

I never have a clever reply to throw back at Bee.

'Did you get it in the neck last night for being late?' Copper Pie asked her. She'd obviously gone round to his. She's always getting told off for not coming home. The thing is she doesn't like going home that much. Her mum and dad have got money problems (Mum says that means no-money problems) and they row all the time (Copper Pie says) and her twin brothers won't leave home because they don't want to do their own washing (Bee says).

'No. Mum was working. Dad was at football. Only the twins were home. We had tea in front of the telly.' (Bee's brothers are really old – more than twenty.)

'That's nice,' said Copper Pie, smiling his wide-mouth-frog smile.

'Is it? I'd rather have your mum yelling and dinner at the table than trays on your lap watching the extreme sports channel.' Bee looked sad. I didn't know what to say. I've never seen the extreme sports channel.

I was saved by the sound of footsteps . . .

'Hey, Jonno,' said Fifty (trying to sound cool).

The five of us stood in a circle in my room.

'Right,' I said. 'I've made a list.'

Copper Pie laughed at me. 'You are *such* a Keener. You can be Tribe secretary.'

'Don't be rude to Keener. He's more use than you are.' Bee was sticking up for me. *Nice.* 'I mean, we don't need a bouncer or a footie freak so what are you going to be?'

Copper Pie stuck his tongue out.

That got us talking about Tribe jobs again. As usual it ended in random lists of nonsense: nose-picker, armpit-smeller, pickpocket, shipwrecker.

I tried to get them to work through my list but it was like trying to do apple-bobbing with no top teeth. After an hour, all we'd managed to decide was the Tribe handshake, which we'd been doing already, and a list of things to do before the next meeting.

Copper Pie was doodling on the cover of my spelling book (he's quite good at drawing but can't write joined up – which is a bit random) when he said, 'Me and Jonno went down the alley after school. Nightmare.'

That's when they told us all about the trouble: their clash with the Alley Cats.

TRIBE JOBS

KEENER: Find container for time capsule and design a Tribe identity card.

FIFTY: Come up with Tribe motto.

COPPER PIE: Look for Tribe den outside school.

BEE: Write manifesto (her idea).

JONNO: Think of missions.

EVERYONE: Think of something important to do like save Black Rhinos (Bee's idea again) or collect cereal box tops.

a true and
faithful account

'We want all the details, leave nothing out,' said Bee. She was in my hammock, swaying. The rest of us were propped up against bits of furniture, except Fifty, who was sitting on my safe.

'I don't want to think about it. I want to *forget* every tiny detail,' said Jonno.

So Copper Pie started, with Jonno chipping in. He called it, 'A true and faithful account of walking home with Jonno,' as though he was in court, which he probably will be one day.

'Bee had gone to the dentist . . . Did you have anything done?'

'No.'

'So the healthy eating's paid off,' said Fifty.

She showed us her teeth.

'Come on, Copper Pie. We want to hear about the Alley Cats,' I said.

'Right,' said Copper Pie. 'Bee had gone, and so had you and Fifty, so there was only Jonno left in the playground . . .' (I was taking notes, just in case anything important cropped up) 'so we went off together.'

'Bee wants details, remember,' said Jonno. 'Copper Pie was eating a sausage roll and he offered me one, but I said no – cold sausage rolls are yuk.'

'Suited me,' said Copper Pie. 'I ate them both. And then we started talking about what we like to eat. And I said I like pork pies with tomato sauce in front of the telly.'

TRIBERS' FAVOURITE FOODS

COPPER PIE: Pork pies, tomato sauce, crisps, meat pie, apple pie, Cornish pasties, sausage rolls, cottage pie, shepherd's pie, chips, scotch eggs, pumpkin pie, blackbird pie, any pie.

BEE: Organic muesli and blueberries.

FIFTY: Anything with loads of sugar.

JONNO: Paella with lots of saffron.

KEENER: Bacon sarnies.

Bee pretended to vomit.

'Can we get on with it?' I said. They were enjoying being

storytellers a bit too much. 'We want details but not *every* word.'

'OK, OK,' said Copper Pie. 'I turned the *right* way – out of the gates towards the bus stop – but Jonno didn't . . . and that was when the trouble started. *He* wanted to go through the alley. I said, "No way".'

'No, you didn't!' said Jonno. 'You said, "Oh no no no no, no," like a girl. So I said, "Oh yes yes yes yes yes" back.'

'Sounds like a pantomime,' I said.

'Exactly what I thought,' said Jonno.

Copper Pie ignored Jonno and carried on as though he wasn't there. 'I tried to tell him to come with me. But he wouldn't.'

'That's because you didn't explain why the alley was such a bad idea,' said Jonno.

'I tried. But you wouldn't have come whatever I said. You'd made your mind up.'

I thought Copper Pie was probably right. It reminded me of the labels his mum has for all the kids she looks after at the nursery: placid (it means dopey), lively (that means headcase), mischievous (pain in the neck) and sensitive (wuss). Jonno's label would be: knows his own mind.

'You told me it was a no-go zone,' said Jonno. 'That was it. End of.'

'That's not true. I told you the kids from the secondary school block it,' said C.P.

'But you didn't say how. And anyway I knew I was safe

with you. I'd been in one of your headlocks, remember? I didn't realise you were *scared*,' said Jonno.

'Did you just say I was scared?' said Copper Pie.

'Yep.' That was brave of Jonno.

THINGS TRIBERS ARE SCARED OF

KEENER: Blood.

BEE: Birds, anything that flaps, or did flap (when it was alive).

COPPER PIE: Celery.

JONNO: Black mambas.

FIFTY: His mum.

'Well, if I was so scared, why didn't I leave you to go down the alley on your own? Answer that.'

'Because you're stupid,' I said. That was brave of me.

'Thanks, Keener.'

'I think he meant loyal,' said Fifty. 'Because you're loyal.'

'I wasn't being loyal or stupid,' said Copper Pie. 'I was stuck with a mate who wouldn't do what I said. What else could I do? I gave in and we went off to the alley. And what a smart move that was, Jonno!'

I hoped they weren't going to fall out.

'But I didn't know what was going to happen, did I?' said Jonno.

'Too right. You were too busy going on about that friend who wants his own Tribe.'

'He's called Ravi,' said Jonno. 'In fact, in the middle of all that, you suddenly asked me if I could sprint. What was that all about?'

'I was working out whether we could leg it if things got tricky, but you said you couldn't run.'

'Oh!' said Jonno. 'I thought it was something to do with Sports Day.'

'Moron,' said Copper Pie.

'We turned into the alley,' said Jonno, avoiding Copper Pie and talking to the rest of us.

The alley is skinny and the walls are high so it's always dark, a bit like our patch. I waited to hear what happened next.

'I was praying *they* wouldn't be there,' said Copper Pie. 'But no such luck. There were loads of them, all hanging about by the bollards at the end.'

'As usual,' said Bee.

'I was totally confused,' said Jonno. 'What could be so frightening about a few girls?'

'I'd forgotten to tell him the gang was all girls,' said Copper Pie. 'But girls are ten times worse than boys. Boys you can thump.'

I agree, I thought. With a sister like Amy I'm an expert on how bad teenage girls can be.

'I didn't get it at all,' said Jonno. 'I kept on walking.'

Inside I was cringing. I could picture the two of them

on their own in the alley – Copper Pie desperate to get away and Jonno with no idea how bad it was going to get.

I looked over at Bee and Fifty. I was sure we were all thinking the same thing. The Alley Cats are witches.

'I wanted to forget it,' said Copper Pie. 'Go back past the bus stop. It was bad enough knowing what they did last time, but this time I was with Jonno who looks . . .'

I knew what Copper Pie meant. Jonno's got mad hair and wears his glasses right at the end of his nose. He walks around with his hands in his pockets, sort of slouchy, and his rucksack hanging so low it nearly drags on the floor. He looks like a brainy American kid, which is fine, except in the alley, where it would be much more useful if he looked like a bodybuilder.

'What do I look like?' said Jonno with a worry crease in his forehead.

Fifty grabbed the glasses, put his hands in his pockets and pretended to walk like Jonno. It was quite funny.

'So what happened next?' I wanted to get to the action (and stop them teasing Jonno).

'Nothing. We kept walking,' said Jonno.

'They'd seen us,' said Copper Pie, 'but they didn't do anything.'

'Until halfway down the alley . . .' added Jonno.

'And?' It was like waiting for Christmas, listening to them plod through the story.

'The girls started clapping.' Jonno showed us: clap-clap,

clap-clap-clap, clap-clap-clap-clap, CLAP-CLAP. 'Like the crowd at football matches. Except instead of shouting "England" they shouted . . . "GINGER!"'

Ouch! Copper Pie wouldn't have liked that.

'I'd have given away my brother – and my mum – to have been watching Ronaldo instead,' groaned C.P.

'You should have legged it,' said Fifty.

'I would have done,' said Copper Pie, 'but *he* didn't want to.'

'Because you had completely failed to explain the danger!' Jonno was getting a bit stressy.

'Stop arguing and get on with it.' How many times was I going to have to hurry them up?

'Don't drop your knitting, Keener,' said Copper Pie.

I stuck my tongue out. So did he.

'Stop it, children,' said Bee.

'OK. There was this girl with really long hair – I think she's the leader – and she started singing . . . about ginger biscuits.'

I let out a small snort. I knew exactly the song Jonno was talking about.

Get back in your biscuit tin, Ginger. Ginger.
Get back in your biscuit tin, Ginger Ginger Nut.

It's *always* Copper Pie's hair they pick on. And it's his hair he's *really* sensitive about.

'I know they were getting at me, but didn't you guess they'd have a go at you next? said Copper Pie.

'I *was beginning* to realise those girls weren't the sort that like skipping and playing dollies,' said Jonno.

'Finally! The penny drops.'

'But I still wasn't scared. I mean, there were some leaning against the walls, some using the bollards as stools and a load standing behind chatting. Not exactly an army ready for action.'

'What did you do?' At last, something was going to happen.

Jonno looked at Copper Pie.

'Jonno went right up to the girls . . . looking pretty cool,' said Copper Pie, 'but when he tried to step over the legs of one of them, she lifted her knee up —'

'And I was left balancing with my leg in the air —'

Copper Pie finished off the sentence. 'Like a stork with too much hair.'

'Thanks,' said Jonno.

'What did she say to you?' said Copper Pie. 'I can't remember.'

'"How's tricks, Frizzy?"'

Fair point, I thought. His hair is totally frizzy.

'And she called you "cute".'

'She did,' said Jonno, squirming.

'And then they all started calling you names, like "Speccy".'

'And they called you "Ginger Puss".'

'I bet they miaowed too,' I said. They're not called the Alley Cats for nothing.

'On the button, Keener,' said Copper Pie. 'They miaowed all right.'

'I tried to get past them again but they all moved and made a wall. I had no idea what to do,' said Jonno.

'And then they started all their rubbish teasing . . .'

Copper Pie and Jonno used squeaky voices to act out the scene.

'Are you late for something? Some cartoon that you like to watch after school? Or do you want to hurry and see your mummy?'

'We haven't seen you before, Frizzy. We'd remember you with that fluffy hair and those cool glasses. Are you Ginger's new friend?'

'Hey Ginger, where's your girlfriend? Has she dumped you?'

'We'll find you a new girlfriend, won't we girls? A nice red-head.'

'And they kept shifting about to stop us barging through,' said Copper Pie. 'But I'd had enough, so I grabbed Jonno's arm, put my head down and we drove through the wall of Alley Cats like we were in a rugby scrum.'

'Did it work?'

'Well, we lived,' said Copper Pie.

'There were hands and feet everywhere but we kept moving,' said Jonno. 'They patted us on the head – no one's done that to me since I was about two! – and tried to trip us up, but Copper Pie wasn't stopping so neither was I. No matter how many ballet pumps were in my way.'

'I'd have ploughed through a brick wall if I'd had to.'

'He would too,' said Jonno.

What the Alley Cats do is torture. They don't beat you up, they tease, like my big sister does. They're crazy. No matter what you do, they embarrass you. They sing, and shout, and dance and clap. Copper Pie would normally stand up for himself with his fists but you can't do that to girls (and I can't do it to anyone). Last time they said Bee was his girlfriend and asked them if they'd kissed. They were both nearly sick.

For once, I was glad I'd had a lift home with Mum!

'You got through, though – that's the main thing,' I said.

'And they all lived happily ever after. The End,' said Fifty.

'Not quite,' said Copper Pie. 'Tell Keener what you said when we stopped running.'

'"Remind me *never* to go that way again."'

'You missed a bit,' said C.P. 'The bit about me being right.'

'You were right, Copper Pie. The alley's a no-go zone, like you said.'

'Is it the end *now?*' I said. My writing hand was about to crumble and fall off like Charles Stratton's ear.

Copper Pie and Jonno exchanged looks.

'The end,' they said. 'Definitely.'

Except of course it wasn't.

Tribe
initiation

Bee threw her legs out of the hammock and stood up.

'Tribers, I hate to say it, but this must be a sign. We need to make the alley safe, not just for us, but for all the kids from school who are scared to set foot on what is a piece of public property. We need to go down the alley. We need to show them that Tribe isn't scared.'

But we are scared, I thought.

'Wow! Some speech,' said Fifty.

'You might be right, Bee,' said Jonno. 'But once was enough. I'm not wild about the alley.'

'Same,' said Fifty.

'Come on, guys. Why should a few big girls stop us from using a short cut home? It's not right.' Bee wasn't going to give in without a fight.

'Well, *I'm* not going down there ever again,' I said.

'Nor me,' said Copper Pie.

'I can't believe you all,' said Bee. 'Sticks and stones and all that. The Cats wouldn't actually hurt us – it's just words. We're in Year 6. Shouldn't we be tough enough to barge past a load of silly girls in silly shoes with pouty lips?'

Jonno moved his head from side to side as though he was weighing it up. 'You're right,' he said.

'As usual,' said Bee.

'But that doesn't mean I want to go back.'

'But you will?'

Jonno nodded.

'What about you, Fifty?'

'If *all* the Tribers agree . . . maybe.'

(*Fifty being brave? What's happening?*)

'Come on, Copper Pie. Surely you're in?' said Bee.

'Nope. Not in.'

Phew! No Copper Pie meant no Fifty and that meant no me.

Or it should have done, but Bee had other ideas. 'Copper Pie, when you're capped for England think how good it'll look when someone digs up our time capsule and finds out about all the amazing things you did when you were a boy. Making the alley safe for all the kids would sound great.'

Surely he wasn't going to fall for that?

Copper Pie spends his life waiting to be discovered by the England trainer and told to leave school *immediately* and kick a ball every day instead. I could almost see the newspaper headline in his eyes: *Goal-scoring genius Copper Pie revealed as schoolboy hero.*

TRIBERS' DREAMS

COPPER PIE: To be the most successful England captain ever.

KEENER: To ban cheese fondue.

BEE: To make lots of money doing something really good for the planet and be interviewed on telly.

JONNO: To discover something that's meant to be extinct, like a dodo.

FIFTY: To grow.

'Do you really think so?' he asked.

'Absolutely,' said Bee.

Absolutely not, I thought. But I said, 'Copper Pie, you can't seriously think we should —'

'I know, I know. But I don't like being pushed around.'

'And what sort of Tribe are we if we let other kids say where we can go and where we can't?' said Jonno.

Help!

Fifty was my only hope. I knew he didn't really want to save the alley . . . but Jonno got there first. 'I've got an idea.'

No, please. Surely they weren't going to make it our next mission.

'Maybe it should be our initiation,' he said. 'A way of being worthy enough to be a member of Tribe.'

'Maybe it should,' said Fifty. 'Initiations are cool.'

'Top idea,' said Copper Pie. 'Blood in. Blood out.'

'What does *that* mean?' I said. I had to know. I can't do blood. If being in Tribe meant blood I'd have to resign. Suddenly being a breath-holder with no friends didn't seem such a bad thing.

'You're sick,' said Bee. 'We're not *that* sort of gang. Don't worry, Keener. They only do the blood thing in comics.'

Phew!

'Think about it,' said Jonno. 'Groups have initiations to test whether you're brave enough or strong enough, or whatever, to join. Going down the alley fits perfectly. We all agreed the Alley Cats shouldn't be allowed to torture everyone. Let's be brave and show them we don't care. If we go together and don't listen to what they say, what's to be scared of?'

'Nothing. We can do it,' said Copper Pie.

'Well said, C.P. You're one brave Triber.' Bee gave him a cheesy smile, and then turned to me.

'Keener, you need to shape up. No wusses in Tribe.'
Thanks, Bee!

'You know *why* he's chicken, don't you?' said Fifty, meaning me.

Jonno shook his head.

```
 ┌─────────────────────────────────────────────┐
 │   SECRETS THAT AREN'T SECRET                  │
 │                                               │
 │   KEENER: Has a crush on Miss Walsh.          │
 │                                               │
 │   COPPER PIE: Can't sleep without Trumpet his │
 │   baby elephant.                              │
 │                                               │
 │   BEE: Sleeptalks whole conversations.        │
 │                                               │
 │   FIFTY: Still fits his age 3-4 Thomas the Tank│
 │   Engine pyjamas.                             │
 │                                               │
 │   JONNO:  It's still a secret.                │
 └─────────────────────────────────────────────┘
```

'Please don't say it,' I pleaded with Fifty. *He wasn't going to rat on me, was he?*

'Keener. We're Tribe now. No secrets. All for one and one for all.'

'Tell us, Fifty,' said Bee.

'They call him "Pinky Prince Charming".'

'Ha ha,' I said, trying to sound like I didn't care, but they were already laughing so it didn't really work. I could feel my face going the Pinky Prince colour.

'Why?' said Jonno. *Did he really need it spelling out?*

'Because that's the colour he always goes when they ask him why he doesn't plait his beautiful long blond hair.'

With friends like mine, who needs enemies! I can't help the way my face behaves and all surfers have long hair and it's not my fault I'm blond. I wished someone would change the subject.

Thankfully someone did – my sister Amy. 'Mum's home,' she yelled. 'She says ten minutes and then it's tea for you and chucking out time for them.'

'OK.'

'Right,' said Bee. 'We've got ten minutes to work out the Tribe initiation.'

a load of
useless ideas

Copper Pie spoke first.

'It's easy. We storm the alley with guns. I've got four – a spud gun, a cap gun, a water pistol and a cowboy gun with a holster that doesn't do anything but looks good.'

Bee and I said, 'No.'

'Same,' said Fifty.

'We can't do that,' said Jonno. 'It'll start a war.'

Copper Pie's eyes lit up.

'We could scare them though, couldn't we?' said Bee. 'We could wear balaclavas and run down the alley shouting. That would scare me.'

'And me,' I said. 'I'd be scared *wearing* a balaclava.'

'Same,' said Fifty. 'And I don't look good in hats, they squash my hair.'

'You're all wimps,' said Copper Pie, but he didn't mean it
. . . I don't think.

'Really we should tell the Head and leave it to her to sort
out,' I said.

Everyone groaned.

'The alley's not school property. She wouldn't do anything,'
said Bee.

'So, apart from storming them, which is unlikely to work,
we've got no ideas,' said Fifty, nicely summing up the situation.

There was a pause while we all had a think (or pretended
to anyway). I was concentrating really hard on a solution that
would make Tribe look good, rather than evil. I hoped the
others were too (except Copper Pie, who can't think 'nice').
Because we'd given ourselves a label, I felt we had to live up to
it. A gang could wear balaclavas and all that, but not Tribe.

'Why do you think they do it?' asked Fifty.

More silence.

Fifty said it again. 'Those girls in the alley, why do you
think they stop everyone and tease them?'

I shrugged to show I wasn't deaf, I just didn't have an
answer.

'Because they can,' said Jonno. 'Because there are loads of
them.'

'There must be fifteen at least,' said Copper Pie. 'That's a
rugby team.'

'Safety in numbers and all that,' said Bee. 'It makes them
brave.'

'Yeah, I bet they wouldn't be so brave on their own.'

Ping. Something that Copper Pie said made a light bulb come on in Jonno's head. It was so obvious we could almost see the light shining through his eye sockets. We waited for him to reveal all.

'Go on, Jonno. We know you've thought of something,' said Fifty.

'Maybe I have,' he said. 'They're brave because there are lots of them. Maybe we could split them up.'

'*Qué?*' said Bee. Another one of her pet expressions. It means 'what' in somewhere she went on holiday.

'Do you know anything about herd behaviour?'

'You mean listening?' I said.

'No. Not "heard" as in ears. We've done ears, remember! "Herd" as in cows.'

'Like "flock",' I said to make it clear I understood.

Every other name for a group came next, not all of them in the dictionary.

TRIBERS' FAVOURITE WORDS FOR GROUPS

- A crash of rhinoceroses
- A murder of crows
- A scrum of Copper Pies (made up by Fifty)
- A flange of baboons
- A prickle of hedgehogs

- A general knowledge of Jonnos
- A library of Keeners (made up by Fifty)
- A parcel of deer
- A nuisance of cats
- An implausibility of gnus
- A bossiness of Bees (Anonymous)
- A runt of Fiftys (also Anonymous)

'Cut,' said Bee, slicing the air with her hand. We shut up.

'So they're a herd of girls and they move in a pack. How does that help?'

'Herds all go the same way, don't they?' said Jonno.

'Tell me something I don't know.' Bee can be horrible sometimes.

'Well, I read somewhere that if one animal splits off in another direction the herd will let him go, but if two animals bolt the herd assumes there's a good reason for it, like a predator they can't see, and they all follow.'

'Thrilling,' said Bee, hands on hips now. 'But we're dealing with girls, not sheep, cows or wildebeest, and there are no predators.'

I butted in. 'Apes and humans are ninety-eight per cent the same.'

'So what you're saying is that we're all sheep?' said Fifty.

'Yes. Most people are sheep because they like following, not leading,' said Jonno. He was quite excited by his idea – but he was the only one.

'What's this biology lesson got to do with the alley?' snapped Copper Pie, who was chucking a scrumpled up pork pie wrapper against my window and trying to catch it.

'Well, if we could get two of the girls to run off, then the others should follow and we could take their place,' said Jonno.

'If we could work out how to get two of them to run, we could get *all* of them to run,' said Bee. 'Forget it.'

'So we're back to weapons,' said you-know-who.

'No,' said Bee. 'You can't walk down an alley and take pot-shots at strangers – even if you're only firing spuds. We'd be arrested.'

'Well, what's your big idea then, bossy?' said Copper Pie.

'Ooooooh!' said Fifty. 'She won't like that.'

'Well, she can lump it because *she* hasn't got an idea.'

'Have so.' Bee obviously hadn't got an idea, but was desperately trying to think of one.

We waited. Copper Pie folded his arms and stared at her.

'Cakes,' she said.

'Is it word association?' said Fifty. 'Icing.'

'Frostbite,' said Jonno.

She did the fringe flick – a sign that she was serious and we were all numbskulls.

'I'll make some cupcakes and we can take them up the alley and give them to the Alley Cats. Everyone loves cupcakes.'

It was so bonkers no one said anything.

'I assume that's agreed then?' She looked around like an

94

auctioneer doing that 'going once, going twice' thing before banging his hammer and shouting 'Sold'. Our time was nearly up.

'No, it's not. We should vote,' said Copper Pie. He pointed his pointing finger at Bee and pretended to pull the trigger. It was getting a bit out of hand. I prefer it when C.P. and Bee are on the same side.

'Fine,' said Fifty. 'Friends, nobles, countrymen —'

'And countrywomen,' added Bee.

'Yes and countrywomen. You have one vote only to choose between baking and warmongering —'

'What about my idea?' said Jonno. No one said anything.

'Actually, all this talking has given *me* an idea,' said Fifty. 'Let's talk to them. Let's go down the alley together and introduce ourselves to the Cats. It's much harder to be rude to someone who's nice to you.'

'I'm bored with this,' said Bee. 'We've got four ideas. Let's vote.'

'Hang on. What about you, Keener? What's your idea?' said Fifty.

Great! Put me on the spot, why don't you?

'Errr . . . we could do what Copper Pie said.'

'Way to go!' shouted C.P. and slapped me on the back.

Quite why I said that I can't tell you. I think it was because Bee called me a wuss. I was fed up with being the one who has to be persuaded into everything. I wanted to be daring for a change. And opting for cupcakes was hardly daring.

'Are you sure, Keener?' asked Bee.

See, she didn't believe me. I shrugged my shoulders.

Copper Pie thumped me again. It would have been less painful if he'd just said, 'Thanks.'

'Two votes for warmongering then.'

What had I done? If everyone else voted for their own idea we would win.

Bee stared hard at Jonno. She moved her lips but *his* mouth spoke.

'Cakes,' it said.

How did she do that?

'Two votes for cakes. Two for war.' Bee grinned.

'Come on, Fifty. Vote for me and I'll look after you. You can have the cap gun.' Copper Pie put his arm round Fifty and ruffled his hair. Fifty loves his black curly hair almost as much as he hates people messing with it. He growled and Copper Pie jumped away pretending to be scared. They like fooling around.

'Nope. I'm voting for myself.'

'I know,' said Jonno. 'How about we do all three?'

'That's nuts. We can't attack them, talk to them and eat cake with them at the same time,' said Fifty.

'We could. It doesn't matter if it's cakes, chat or squirting with water and bombarding with potatoes, as long as it stops them singing songs about us.'

'He's got a point.' Bee looked round at the rest of us.

'Sounds good to me. I'll be a good team player and follow

Captain Jonno's orders.' Copper Pie saluted at Jonno and stamped his foot.

'Me too,' I said. Glad that I wasn't going to be sent down the alley waving a cowboy gun with only Copper 'The Maniac' Pie by my side.

'Same,' said Fifty.

'Since when have I been Captain?' said Jonno. 'Since when has there even *been* a captain?'

He looked really cross. We all looked at each other. We'd obviously done something wrong, but weren't sure what.

He carried on. 'I thought all Tribers were equal. That's what you said, Keener.'

There was a delay in my brain transmitters so Fifty spoke for me. 'I think Copper Pie just called you Captain because you're the one who has good ideas.'

'No, I'm not.' Jonno shook his head. 'My idea about herds was rubbish. Bee said so.'

I'm sure the others felt every bit as confused as I did. I'd have loved someone to call *me* Captain. *What was going on?*

'Well, it *was* rubbish, but your idea to put everything together isn't,' said Bee. 'It's clever.'

'You don't get it, do you? Firstly, it's no good having ideas if you don't have anyone else to have them with. Secondly, ideas just pop up. Anyone can have them. I only had my idea because you all had yours. Thirdly, you don't know me. You only met me four days ago. You don't know that without you, I wouldn't dare do anything.'

He looked a bit odd. Not Jonno-like at all. Smaller . . .

'But you invaded our territory and didn't budge even when we all stood against you. You dared to do that,' said Fifty.

'Only because I had to.' His bottom lip was sticking out a tiny bit. Flo's does that when she doesn't get her own way (and so does Fifty's sometimes).

'What d'you mean?' said Copper Pie.

'Let's just say I wouldn't recommend moving to a new school when everyone's already made their friends. The only kids who ever want to be friends with a new boy are the weirdos who've never had a friend because they're seriously strange. Trust me, I'm an expert. So you either stick it out on your own and wait for someone to notice you're human or you do it my way – work out which of the kids couldn't care less whether there's a new kid or not because they've already got friends. *They're* the normal ones. That's why I chose you lot, because you didn't need any more friends.'

It was quite hard to follow. He chose to be friends with the people who didn't want to be friends with him, because the ones who want to be friends with a new boy are saddos with no friends.

I worked it out just in time to hear the last bit of Jonno's speech.

'I don't want to be *Captain*. I'm just happy not to be Jonno-no-friends.' He sighed.

(Can you believe that on his first day Jonno looked round

the classroom and chose *us* to be friends with? That made me feel pretty good.)

'Jonno, you've offended us now,' said Bee in an upset voice with eyes to go with it.

Poor Jonno. All he'd done was admit he wanted us to be friends and now Bee was angry . . .

'How dare you call us normal!' She smiled an enormous magazine-cover smile and gave his arm a squeeze and we all started to laugh. It wasn't really that funny but we were all relieved that she was only teasing.

TRIBERS' EMBARRASSING MOMENTS

KEENER: Fell asleep sucking his thumb on the way back from a school trip to the museum.

BEE: Put her hand up in assembly to ask Mr Morris a question and accidentally called him 'Dad'.

JONNO: Every time he starts a new school

FIFTY: Knows all the words to *The Sound of Music* and sang along when we watched it at school.

COPPER PIE: The sleepover when Keener found Trumpet the elephant under C.P.'s pillow

---

We didn't get a chance to talk about how the Tribe initiation

Treats, Talk or Torture (Fifty came up with that) was actually going to work because Fifty and Bee went off to play with Flo, who was mattress surfing. (She drags the spare mattress up the stairs to the top landing, piles all her favourite cuddly toys on it and then slides down. It always ends in tears because the cuddlies fall off, or Flo does.)

'You wouldn't be sliding on that mattress again, would you, Flo?' shouted Mum. 'Not after the banister nearly dislocated your elbow.'

'No, Mummy,' shouted Flo. 'Keener's friends are doing it.'

We did the Tribe handshake: one, two, three, and then everyone legged it.

'I've got a lot to get ready,' said Copper Pie.

They'd decided to attack the alley the next day. I didn't remember agreeing but . . .

'And I need to get cake-making.'

Bee makes incredibly delicious cakes. She can cook all sorts of things. Her dad and her brothers don't do anything in the kitchen. Bee complains because boys should learn to cook too but her mum doesn't agree. Neither do I. I'd much rather eat them.

I had hoped that Fifty would stay behind because we had a problem . . . Going down the alley after school wasn't going to be easy if I was on the way home in the back of the car with Flo, and Fifty was with his mum and Probably Rose. We needed to invent a reason why we didn't need picking up.

It was strange that I hadn't heard his mum come to get

him. I looked out of my bedroom window in case he was waiting outside. Nope. I was about to check downstairs when I noticed a Fifty-sized shape quite far up the street walking along with Jonno (I could tell by the hair). No mums in sight.

That decided me. We'd talked about it for long enough. If Fifty had somehow managed to persuade his mum to let him walk around on his own, then it was time I stood up to my mum. If you're prepared to confront an alley full of girls, all older than you, then dealing with your own mum can't be that hard. I thought I'd try and find that Keener of Tribe voice again – the one that was a bit louder.

As I was in a deciding mood, I decided something else too. Rather than lying in bed worrying about Treats, Talk or Torture, which is what I would usually do, I thought I'd try something Fifty's mum had suggested. (Her job is to do with making people think differently so that they're happier or richer or have less headaches or something.) She said that when I hear the voice in my head saying worrying things, I could remind myself that it's not real, it's just worry. The voice could just as easily say good things, or sing, or say rubbish words like 'compodasty'.

Worrying makes no difference to whether things turn out right or not.

I made up loads of excellent rubbish words after that and totally forgot to worry.

My favourite rubbish word: 'flimflog'.

treats, talk
or torture

I walked to school on my own. Not with Fifty. Not with anyone. Result! It happened at breakfast:

Me: 'Mum, I want to start walking to school and back.'

Mum: 'I think it's marvellous that you want to be independent, and of course the exercise would do you good, but —'

Me: 'I know all the reasons but I'm Year 6. I'm sensible. And I don't want to be the only one of my friends who has to go with his mum.'

Amy: 'Let him, Mum.'

Mum: 'If you'd both let me finish. I was about to say that I've spoken to Fifty's mum and we agreed it was time, BUT to start with, I'd like you to text me when you get there and make sure you're home by half past four.'

Me: 'Oh!'

Amy: 'Is that all you can say?'

Me: 'Can I start today?'

Mum nodded.

Amy: 'There's something you're missing, bro.' She put her hand up, thumb by her ear, little finger by her mouth.

Me: 'Mum, I don't have a phone.'

Mum: 'Tomorrow's Saturday. I thought you could drag your dad to the shops after your swimming lesson.'

Flo: 'I want a phone. Why can't I have a phone? It's not fair. I'm always last . . .'

That's when I left. It was so cool striding out of the door on my own. I was already choosing my phone. One of those phones that slides open and plays music, so I can walk along with earphones. And a ringtone that no one else has got.

Copper Pie was hanging around by the school gates. He had a huge plastic bag, the sort they give you in toy shops.

'Keener! How come you're walking?'

'Mum's finally realised I can cross roads *and* refuse lifts from strangers. And because she wants me to be safe, I'm getting my own phone.'

'If she wants you to be safe she should have gone for a Desert Eagle, best semi-automatic pistol ever made —'

'Why do you say stupid things like that?' said Bee's voice, before I spotted her body.

'Because he's stupid, of course,' said Fifty, from behind Bee.

'Who's stupid?' asked Jonno as he came through the gates.

'Last one to the den is,' said C.P. sprinting off with no chance of it being him. Last one there was Bee, probably because she was carrying a cake tin!

I hadn't had much to do with Callum (public enemy number one) since term started. He stays away from us because we've got a not-so-secret secret weapon – Copper Pie.

So at morning break, the last thing I was expecting was his ugly face poking through the branches while we were trying to plot the after-school assault (or hopefully tea party) in the alley.

'Hello,' he shouted.

We all stopped talking.

'Carry on. Don't mind me,' he said.

'What d'you want, Hog?' Copper Pie calls him that because he never passes the ball. Instead of wanting the team to win, all he wants is to be the one who scores.

'Callum. The name is Callum.'

'Callum, it's private, OK?' said Bee. 'So push off.'

'Stressy. I'm watching you. That's all I wanted to say. I'm

watching you.' And then he was gone.

'What did he mean?' asked Jonno.

'Nothing. He's an idiot,' I said.

'A clever idiot who we should be wary of, or an idiot idiot?'

I thought for a minute. 'Ummm . . . a clever idiot, I suppose. He sucks up to teachers. He controls most of the games in the playground – you know, says who can play and who can't, decides what they do . . . He's almost as fast a runner as Copper Pie here.'

'Remember the "almost", it's important,' said Copper Pie.

'And he doesn't like you?' said Jonno.

'He's never bothered us and we don't bother him,' said Fifty. 'But . . . perhaps he doesn't like Tribe.'

'He doesn't know about Tribe,' I said.

'He may not know we're Tribe,' Fifty went on, 'but he knows there are five of us now and that we're always together. Maybe he thinks we're plotting a coup. *Playground Tsar's reign of terror ended by secret tribe.*'

'Now you're talking, Fifty. Maybe we *should* take over,' said Copper Pie, rubbing his hands together.

'*Wicked gangmaster toppled by Tribe.* Sounds good,' said Bee.

'One thing at a time,' said Jonno. 'The alley, then Callum.'

It was as if he knew we were up to something. Back on our patch after the dullest history lesson ever (plotting towns

TRIBE

with 'chester' or 'cester' in their names on a map of England to show where the Roman forts were), we were about to decide the details of Tribe's Treats, Talk or Torture initiation when his ugly mug popped up again.

'What's in the bag?' he asked.

Copper Pie was guarding it with his life. He'd kept it by him all day. Guns aren't allowed in school.

'The body of the last person to bother me, Hog.'

'Wouldn't be a weapon, would it?'

I made a how-did-he-know face at Fifty. Fifty made a we're-done-for face at me.

'So I'm right,' said Callum.

Bee rolled her eyes at us and made a give-it-away-why-don't-you face.

Sorry, I wanted to say.

'If you start making trouble for me . . .' Copper Pie stepped towards Callum.

'Don't bother with him,' said Jonno. 'If he really thinks we'd be stupid enough to bring a . . . I don't know . . . a gun, or a bow and arrow to school, then it's his duty to go and report us. Off you go, Callum.'

He went. Jonno has that effect on people.

'What did you say that for?' said Fifty. 'Everyone knows Copper Pie is stupid enough to bring a gun.'

'I am not,' said C.P.

Bee pointed at the bag.

'I am,' he said.

Bee started laughing. They all joined in, but I couldn't see what was funny about being caught with a bag of guns, even if they were harmless.

'I don't think Callum will risk telling on us,' said Bee. 'I mean . . . there might be a weapon in the bag, there might not.'

'Let's hope you're right,' I said. But what I wanted to say was: *To make absolutely sure he doesn't tell, we could let Copper Pie biff Callum a little bit . . .*

Thanks to Callum's interference, the only time left to sort things out was while we ate lunch, before Copper Pie had to take up his position on the naughty chair.

'Well?' said Fifty.

No one was talking. Everyone was chewing.

'Come on. What are we going to do?'

Bee sighed. 'I suppose *I'd* better start us off. Right, we'll walk up the alley together, ignoring all the chanting, teasing, whatever . . .'

'OK,' said Fifty.

'And then . . .'

You could see that Bee's brain was busy but nothing was coming through.

Silence. Even Jonno seemed stumped. I don't know why I always expect him to be the one to come up with something. After all, he's just a boy, like me, except a bit cooler, slightly more interesting and . . .

'How about you get a cake for every shot you dare fire?' said Copper Pie.

'Have you been listening at all, Der-brain?' said Bee. 'The cakes aren't a reward for us. They're a bribe for them. Honestly!' She gave him a withering look and he withered a bit, but tried again.

'We could shoot them with cakes instead of potatoes. Aim into their mouths.'

'Shut up, Copper Pie,' said everyone (except me).

Because I, that is me, Keener, had got an idea. And it couldn't be worse than one of his. I opened my mouth and let the words tumble out.

'It's simple. Fifty can go first because he's in charge of talking. He can explain that we want them to stop the name-calling so we can use the alley whenever we like. Then Copper Pie can show them his arsenal and then Bee can step in and say that we'd rather share our cakes than be enemies.'

Made sense to me.

'Makes sense to me,' said Fifty. I'm sure he heard my thought.

'Let's hope they choose cakes,' said Jonno. 'What if they choose war?'

I was so pleased with myself I thought I'd try again.

'If they choose war we could start at the beginning again and Fifty could explain why war wouldn't be good for them or us, and then we could try the cakes again.'

108

'It's all down to you then, Fifty,' said Bee.

He creased his forehead.

'Don't worry, I'll be right behind you,' said Copper Pie. 'Just say the word and I'll have my telescopic gun-sight trained on them.'

'You wish.' Fifty laughed.

'So is that it then?' said Jonno.

Everyone was staring at me because it was my idea. I hesitated. I knew I should say, 'Yes, that's the plan', in a confident manner. But what if it failed . . .?

'Yes, that's it,' said Bee.

She clicked her fingers on both hands (I wish I could do that) and stood up. 'I'm going to catch the Head. Tell her I've looked at the Earth Day website before she changes her mind about *Go Green*.'

She was gone, leaving her tray. I tidied it away for her.

'Oh well, time to babysit the Head's naughty chair.'

Copper Pie got up and grabbed the bag from under his seat.

'Better leave that with us, idiot,' said Fifty.

We hung around under the trees, looking after the bag. I couldn't help thinking it would have been better if he'd put the guns in his kit bag or a rucksack. Or hidden them under a bush and picked them up after school. I kept expecting sparks and bangs, like fireworks.

Jonno was picking the bark again. 'Look, I think it might be a longhorn beetle.'

'That's too little to be a long anything,' said Fifty.

Jonno didn't take any notice. 'There are loads of things that live under the bark: cobweb beetles, weevils . . .'

They had a great long conversation about all the grubs and bugs in our area, but I only half listened. I was wondering where Callum was. He definitely wasn't in the playground.

Maybe he was waiting outside the staffroom, ready to rat on us about the 'weapons'?

CONVERSATION BETWEEN
CALLUM AND HIS DEPUTY, JAMIE

Callum: I don't like the way Copper Pie's lot have joined up with that kooky new kid.

Deputy: Nor me, Cal.

Callum: Have you seen that plastic bag they're lugging around everywhere?

Deputy: I have, Cal.

Callum: What d'you think's in it?

Deputy: Don't know, Cal.

Callum: Well, find out then.

Deputy: How can I do that, Cal?

Callum: I don't know. But I want to know what's in that bag.

Deputy: Got it, Cal.

Callum: What you waiting for then?

happy
birthday!

Why was Callum's dozy deputy, Jamie West, standing by me in the line-up for afternoon school?

'What's in the bag, Keener?'

I tightened my hand round the bunched up plastic. *How come I'd ended up with the loot?*

'Get back in your kennel,' said Fifty.

'I'm not a dog,' said Jamie.

'Why do you go around on the end of Callum's lead then?'

I wished Fifty would shut up. It was *my* sweaty hand that was holding the bag of guns!

Jonno was in the loo so it was only the two of us. We were no match for Jamie. If he grabbed the bag we were finished.

Or were we?

'Hey Jamie,' shouted Bee, running across the play-

112

ground. 'You don't mind if I push in, do you?'

She elbowed her way past him.

'Do you want something?' she asked him.

He was going to answer but she interrupted before he got the first word out. 'No? Well, why don't you go somewhere you're wanted then?' She nodded towards the front of the queue where Callum was standing with his back to us.

Where did he pop up from?

'Show me what's in the bag and I'll go.'

'No can do. It'll ruin the surprise.'

'What surprise?'

'Do you promise you won't tell?'

'Promise,' he said.

Don't tell him, Bee, said the voice in my head.

She whispered in his ear.

'Really?' he said.

She nodded. He grinned (not something you see often), and went to report back to Callum.

'What did you say?' Fifty asked

'You didn't tell him we had —'

Bee cut me off. 'Do you think I'm stupid?'

We both shook our heads.

She moved the black hair away from her eyes and looked at us as though she was our nursery teacher and we were three again.

'I told Jamie that it's Jonno's birthday today and we've bought in a piñata for end of school but not to say anything because we haven't asked Miss Walsh yet. Satisfied?'

It was a good lie. Piñatas come in all sorts of weird shapes, like donkeys and stars, and the stick you whack them with to get the sweets out would explain the pokey bit made by Copper Pie's longest gun.

'An excellent lie, Bee. Top marks for being dishonest. You should try it more often,' said Fifty.

She stuck her tongue out at him.

The afternoon seemed to go on forever. I'm not sure what I was more worried about: offering cakes to the Alley Cats or Callum and Jamie demanding a piñata after school. Luckily I remembered that I could make the voice in my head say whatever I like.

The crocodile in my pocket likes bubblewrap.

In between making up my silly sentences (I was meant to be reading), I heard a 'Psst!' It was Fifty. Using sign language he managed to say: 'Meet at the end of the alley straight after school.'

I did a thumbs up in return.

(That gave me another good idea for Tribe – our own set of signs for sending messages.)

I put everything away in my desk, apart from my book, so that I was ready for the bell. I wanted to make sure I wasn't last, just in case.

Finally, the bell went.

'Right, class,' said Miss Walsh. 'Don't forget that I want

you to bring in as many newspapers as you can next week, because we're going to build bridges. And Jonno, could you stay behind for a minute?'

Disaster! No. He can't stay behind. Definitely not. No.

I tried frantically to catch someone's eye, but Bee and Copper Pie and Fifty were all too busy catching each others' and I kept missing.

I didn't know what to do. Should I dash to the alley like Fifty said, or wait for Jonno and hope he could talk to Miss Walsh and still get out without Callum singing 'Happy Birthday' and demanding his swipe at the donkey or whatever?

I put my rucksack on and waited for a sign.

Jonno weaved his way to the front, past Copper Pie, who immediately upped and left, past Bee, who followed dragging Fifty with her and finally to me.

'Go,' he said.

Knowing me, you'd think I'd have been relieved, but I found myself not wanting to leave Jonno on his own. *Courage. Very strange.*

'Shall I wait in the corridor?' I whispered.

'No. Go.'

Callum and Jamie were already hanging around by Miss Walsh's desk. They were obviously determined to get a share of the sweets. I couldn't see any way Jonno could escape without trouble.

'Get a move on, Keener.'

It was Copper Pie's voice coming from the gap in the doorframe.

As soon as I was through the door, I was swept up and propelled along the corridor and down the stairs by my ginger friend. I tried to dig my heels in but he's stronger than me.

'Let go! I want to wait for Jonno.'

'Why?'

'In case he . . . needs help.'

Copper Pie stopped dead and I kept going and banged into him.

'What help are *you* gonna be?'

'Thanks,' I said. It's nice to know what your friends think of you!

'See you at the alley then. If you make it.'

I didn't need Copper Pie to say that. I was already regretting my decision. But I'd said I'd wait. So I did. I crept back up to where we hang our stuff, climbed up on to the bench and burrowed into a couple of old coats that had been there since the winter, or maybe the winter before.

I could hear talking but not the words because there were too many people still in the classroom.

Alice came out. Then Rose. Then Archie.

I stayed very still and tried to look like part of the coat – if it works for an egg-box-ear, why shouldn't it work for me? I didn't want to have to answer any questions about why I was loitering.

Tom. Molly.

Come on, Jonno.

The longer I waited, the hotter I got. And the hotter I got, the more panicky I felt.

Joe. Roddy. Jack.

There can't have been many kids left.

I wanted to peep but the thought of coming face to face with an angry Callum put me off.

Come on, Jonno.

I was feeling a bit faint. The coat was itchy against my neck and the hood had worked its way down over my forehead so I couldn't see properly.

'*Happy birthday to you . . .*' Oh no! Miss Walsh's voice was like a loudspeaker. More voices joined in, all singing to the birthday boy. You see, that's what happens when you tell lies. One lie leads to another – my mum always says that.

'*Happy birthday, dear Jo-nno. Happy Birthday to you.*'

A flash of big hair and specs ran past the coats. *What's happening?* I leapt down off the bench and raced after it. The coat came with me but there was no time to sort it out. I had to get away before Callum and Jamie realised there was no piñata and no birthday. My heart was doing that boom boom thing. I didn't dare turn round. I ran as fast as I could after Jonno's feet. I couldn't see the rest of him because half my face was blindfolded by the hood. Thankfully, somewhere between the bottom of the stairs and the outside door it lost its grip and slid off, just in time for me to swerve round Mr Dukes and pile out into the playground. I dodged a game of football and jumped over a pile of girls' bags. The path was clear after that so I picked up speed.

I caught up with him at the gates where he'd stopped for a second. I checked behind. There was no sign of Callum or Jamie. *Phew!*

Neither of us spoke. We were both panting so it wasn't really an option. Jonno tilted his head in the direction of the alley and we were off again.

In front of us we could see the other Tribers. They were clapping.

'We'd almost given up hope,' said Bee.

'What took you?' asked Copper Pie.

'Well done,' said Fifty. 'I thought Treats, Talk or Torture might have to be postponed.'

Something about the plastic look on his face made me think that was what he was hoping for.

'Are you all right, Keener?' Bee asked me. My face was burning so I knew it must be bright red . . .

'You're purple,' said Copper Pie.

. . . or purple.

'Thanks.' I started frantically blowing upwards to try and make my face a normal colour before I had to face the Alley Cats.

'So, what happened?' asked Bee. 'You obviously got away without Callum trying to hit you with a stick to get the sweets out of you.'

118

'Only just,' said Jonno. 'Miss Walsh said she hoped I'd enjoyed my first week. I didn't have time to answer because Callum interrupted and told her it was my birthday.'

'Nice one, Callum!' said Copper Pie.

'He also told her that we were having a piñata. I pretended to be shocked. Like this.'

Jonno opened his mouth wide and made his eyes all goggly.

'So how did you get away?' asked Bee.

'I waited while they sang "Happy Birthday" to me and then said I was going to find the piñata.'

'And?' Bee's not very patient.

'And I ran away.'

'Cool,' said Fifty. 'You left them waiting for the invisible piñata. They're probably still there.'

'But what about you, Keener?' said Bee. 'Copper Pie said you stayed behind to help. We didn't believe him, of course.'

'Well, you should have. I hid in the coats and waited for Jonno.'

'There you go, Bee. Wrong again,' said Jonno, winking.

'I apologise,' said Bee. 'And declare that you, Keener, are officially no longer a wuss.'

'Thank you.' I bowed my head as if I was being knighted. Keener of Tribe, OBE.

'Come on, then,' I said. 'Initiation time. Let's all prove ourselves worthy of the name "Triber".'

I took a step towards the alley.

facing
the mob

We turned into the alley, all five of us in a row. At one end there was Bee, holding the cake tin. Next, Copper Pie in charge of the plastic bag. Then me, Fifty and Jonno. A line of Tribers.

We looked straight ahead at the familiar sight – an alley full of girls, lolling about, laughing and chatting.

What did we think we were doing? Never again, we'd all said. The alley was out of bounds. Why were we bothering? Did we need an initiation? Couldn't we be Tribers without being brave?

Because of all the trouble with Callum, I hadn't had much time to worry about the alley. But standing there, not knowing what was going to happen, was super-stressy. I tried to stay calm by imagining the girls were big versions of

Flo, but she's quite scary so it wasn't one of my best ideas. Keener the Brave was shrinking back into Keener the Not-so-Brave, at speed.

I took a breath and felt Fifty do the same. I could tell he was nervous about his role in the initiation. Who wouldn't be? He had to do all the talking. I was glad I'd sided with Copper Pie – I was fairly sure I could leave all the gun stuff to him.

We made our way, slowly, down the alley.

'When do I speak, Keener?' said Fifty in a sort of quiet hiss.

Why was he asking me? I waited for someone else to answer . . .

Bee reached across and nudged me. 'Tell him, Keener.'

I don't know, I thought. *I'm not in charge.*

'It's your plan. You're in charge.'

I swear they hear my thoughts.

There was complete silence. I didn't even try and make a plan. I thought about Flo who was at home probably having a piece of chocolate cake and a drink of blackcurrant and wished I was too.

'Hey look, girls! Our friends have come to play.'

The Alley Cats turned round to stare at us. I stopped walking. The rest of the Tribers did the same. Being in charge was horrendous. I vowed I'd never have an idea ever again.

'Frizzy! Back so soon. Did you miss us?'

'And Ginger Puss. Miaow.'

'It's the Pinky Prince too. And Ginger's girlfriend.'

'And Titch. Shouldn't you be at nursery?'

I could feel the Tribers' eyes on me. I had to do something. We were like skittles standing in a line, waiting to be knocked over.

'Now, Fifty. Now,' I said and pushed him in front of us.

He stood there and wound one of his curls round his finger, which is something he used to do when he was little.

'Have you got something to say, Titch? Go on, don't be afraid.'

'Hi,' he said. It came out a bit squeaky. 'We, er . . . we wondered . . .'

'I think he's trying to ask you for a date, Sass.'

Sass, the one with the hair down to her knees, stood up and smiled at Fifty. It was scary.

'I'd love to go out with you, Titch. You're so cute but —'

'Stop it!' Fifty shouted.

The girls started to laugh.

'I mean it.'

Poor Fifty. It was a disaster. They were never going to listen to him. I looked across at Jonno, hoping he was going to magic up some way of us *not* looking like complete idiots. He looked straight back at me.

Copper Pie nudged me . . . a bit too hard. 'Ow!'

'Oh Pinky! Did Ginger hurt you?' the Sass girl said.

As she came towards us, she threw all her blond hair to

one side so it was hanging over her shoulder. She looked like Rapunzel. A few of the others followed her.

THINGS WRONG WITH RAPUNZEL, THE FAIRY TALE

Rapunzel was locked in a tall tower by a witch. There was no key and no door. (So how did she get in there then?)

The witch climbed up Rapunzel's ridiculously long hair. (Why didn't she use her broom?)

One day a handsome prince came. (An ugly prince would have been less predictable.)

He climbed up her hair too and they fell in love. (She wouldn't have fallen in love with someone who had pulled her hair because it hurts.)

The witch tricked the prince. He fell and was blinded. (He'd have died – it was a tall tower remember?)

Rapunzel escaped and found him begging. Her tears gave him back his sight. They all lived happily ever after. (Not true – the witch didn't.)

Oh help!

Everyone knows mobs are dangerous. Even if in real life they're ballet teacher or baby-minders, put a load of people together and they'll start fighting. We could be beaten to a pulp. And pulp means blood and gore.

I was clear about one thing – if they came any closer we were going to have to abandon the initiation. If we failed, we'd just have to put up with being unworthy of belonging to Tribe. I could cope with that.

'What's brought your little gang here today then, Pinky?'

She was talking to me. I could feel my face getting warm all over again. She was looking *straight* at me. It was definitely a moment for some of Fifty's mum's magic.

I gave myself a lecture inside my head.

Pinky . . . That's just a word. Like 'bubblewrap'. It can't hurt me. And neither will they. They're teasing, like Amy does, because they're older than us.

She waited for me to answer.

I waited to see if I had anything else to say to myself . . .

Nope, the lecture seemed to be over. I took a deep breath.

'Actually, we're not a gang. We're Tribe,' I said.

It came out pretty good. Loudish. Not squeaky. No one laughed at me. I checked behind – Jonno made a carry-on sign with his eyes.

So I carried on. 'And we'd like to come down the alley without you lot shouting at us.'

Good stuff, I thought.

'Ahh! Bless. We've scared them,' she said, looking round at her mates. I was getting ready to say the guns and cakes bit (I was, honest) when Bee barged past me with the tin.

'It's simple. We've got weapons in there . . .' She turned

124

round and pointed at the bag. Copper Pie did an evil grin. 'Or we've got cakes.' She opened the tin.

You should have seen their faces. It was like happy dust had been sprinkled all over them. The girls all whooped, and ahh-ed and wowee-ed. I could see why. Bee had made about thirty cakes, all with different coloured icing and flowers made of pink and white marshmallow petals with Smarties for the middles. They looked amazing.

'Did *you* make those?'

Bee nodded.

'For us?'

'Yes, but only if you agree to stop being bullies.' She'd used the b-word. That wasn't going to go down well.

The main girl, Sass, didn't say anything right away. She turned round to face her mates.

It was like waiting to find out whether you were guilty, and about to be sent to the dungeons, or free to go.

Was she going to make a deal? Cakes for peace.

Or would she choose combat?

Or, worst of all, would they snatch the cakes from us but carry on teasing anyway?

I didn't move or breathe. I don't think my heart was beating either. Out of the corner of my eye, I could see Copper Pie swinging the bag slightly, as though he didn't want her to forget what was in it. Like a threat. Nothing else moved.

Why was she taking so long? 'So what do you think?' she

said to the rest of them.

I heard some mumbles but they didn't make words.

Come on.

She slowly swivelled back round.

'Well . . .'

I took a step back. I couldn't help it. If they were going to attack I didn't want to be in the front line.

I think she knew what I was thinking. It happens to me a lot. Maybe my thoughts are very loud.

I don't see why someone being scared of you is funny, but she obviously thought it was. Her mouth curved up at the corners and she laughed.

'I say we go for cakes. What do you think, girls?'

'Definitely.'

'For sure.'

'NO WAY!'

Oh no! Who said that?

'Only joking. I'm for cakes.'

They all agreed. *Fantastic! No war.*

We watched Bee offer round the cakes. Everyone took one. And then it was our turn. And it was totally weird. I don't think any of us felt even a tiny bit scared of the Alley Cats. You can't hang around eating a cake with yellow icing and a pink flower with a blue Smartie middle and be frightened of someone standing by you eating a cake with green icing and a white flower with a red Smartie middle. You just can't.

It reminded me of that story about how the Germans and the English had a ceasefire on Christmas Day. One minute they were fighting and the next they were sharing their dinner and singing carols.

THE CHRISTMAS TRUCE

In World War I there were loads of German and English soldiers fighting in the trenches. On Christmas Eve 1914 both sides had been sent supplies like plum puddings and miniature Christmas trees but they couldn't enjoy them because of the war. The front lines of each army were close enough to shout across, so some of the soldiers decided to call a ceasefire. Amazingly, they even climbed out of the trenches and joined each other in No Man's Land, sharing food and drink and singing carols like 'Silent Night'. After Christmas Day they went back to being enemies.

By the time we'd eaten all the cakes (Copper Pie had three), Bee had agreed to meet the Cats the next day with the recipe written out, including how to do the decorating.

Sass had said she was sorry. 'No more teasing, we promise. Everyone is welcome in the alley.'

Copper Pie had shown his collection of toy guns and even let some of the girls have a go.

And Jonno had explained about Tribe and the initiation. They were all really interested, even though they're at secondary school.

'Being a Tribe sounds really wicked,' said Sass. 'Can I join?'

'No, sorry,' said Jonno.

'Only joking,' she said and gave him a sort of squeeze.

Jonno suddenly found something interesting to look at on the floor.

'So where did you get the kooky idea to do cakes or war?'

We all did different versions of a shrug.

So Fifty spoke. 'Well . . . Bee likes cooking and Copper Pie likes guns.'

'I thought you were going to say something really clever,' said Sass.

'Like what?' asked Bee.

'Well, they say everything people do is because of love or fear. That's like cakes or war, isn't it? Love cakes. Fear war.'

I thought about that. It made sense. Tribe had made a good choice, even if it was accidental.

'Time we were off,' said Sass. 'See you then, Tribers. And thanks for the cakes. Awesome.'

As Sass walked off with some of the others, Bee said, 'I'm going to grow my hair that long.'

Girls!

Copper Pie put out his hand. I slapped mine on top. The noise made Sass turn round. She watched as Jonno and Bee and Fifty added theirs. We shouted, 'One. Two. Three,' and threw our hands in the air.

'Is that a Tribe thing?' shouted Sass.

'Yep,' said Copper Pie.

'Cool,' she yelled.

'Yeah, it is,' we shouted back.

late
home

Bee was full of it on the way home.

'We freed the alley. All the kids can use it now. Yeah!' She punched the air.

She said that the reason Tribe succeeds is because we believe in it. We're still the same kids we were before but, because of Tribe, we're powerful. It's made us different.

'So what shall we do next?' she said. 'Now that we've proved ourselves.'

'Go home and have tea,' said Copper Pie. 'Initiations make you hungry.'

'Not possible. You're full of cake,' she said. 'Seriously, guys, what's our next job?'

'Bee, we can't expect to change something every day,' said Fifty.

'Why not?'

'Because we'd be too tired,' he said and we all laughed.

'What's next,' said Jonno, 'is explaining to Miss Walsh that we got my birthday wrong.'

'When is your birthday?' asked Fifty.

'October eleventh. We were only six months too early.'

'Easy mistake to make,' said Fifty.

At the end of the high street, Fifty and I went straight on and the others went left.

'Bye,' we all shouted.

The turn to Fifty's house is before mine so I walked the last part on my own. I had lots to think about. I knew what Bee meant about being in Tribe. It was like wearing armour or being given a lion's heart. My mind wandered, like it does in dreams. I thought about a tribe in South America that Jonno told me about that doesn't have a word for 'worry', so no one worries. That would suit me. They don't have words for numbers either, so Copper Pie would like it because there's no counting. And I thought about how good it is now there are five of us. And about how Copper Pie is the Triber I've known the longest because he saved me from Annabel Ellis at nursery.

'The agreement was that you would walk straight home. I have been sitting here with Flo trying not to worry. The first day you're allowed to . . .'

Mum went on and on but nothing went in. I stared at

the evil grin on my nasty little sister's face. She loves trouble, as long as she's not in it.

Scowl away, Flo, I'm so not bothered.

When Mum finally stopped I said, 'Sorry', went up to my room and laid in my hammock.

What a great day! Nothing could take away the feeling, not even Mum's telling off.

So she didn't know what had come over me . . .

So I was acting out of character . . .

Exactly, I wanted to say.

Surely new me was better than old me. I realised I hadn't held my breath for days. I hadn't had any bad dreams either. I felt like a snake, who'd shed its skin and started again as . . .

Keener of Tribe – full of good ideas, not wet blanket.

Keener of Tribe – trailblazer (of the route to school and back).

Keener of Tribe – warrior, not worrier.

Could it get any better?

Bribes,
Beetles,
Bark
and
Bobotie

being
a Triber

It's funny how quickly exciting things become normal.
When I first got my phone I was always changing ringtone
and texting and playing the games but now . . . I'm still glad
I've got one, but it's not like when it was new. It's the same
with walking home. I felt so grown up the first few times but
now it's just part of a regular school day.

Being a Triber is normal too. We meet once a week
(Wednesdays) at my house because:

Fifty's mum's too nosy so we can't go there.

Jonno says his dad doesn't like other people's kids.

Bee likes everyone else's house better than hers,
and everyone's scared of Copper Pie's mum. (She shouts.)

We'd like somewhere else to meet, like a proper hut,
but no one's got one. We might build one. Fifty's garden

is huge and messy. He's done a deal with his mum: if we clear the bottom of it, which is a jungle of nasty pointy bushes and junk and smelly stuff, then we can have a go. Copper Pie wanted to do it right away but it's not really a couple-of-nights-after-school type of job. My dad said 'Maybe we could do it one weekend,' but he needs to talk to Fifty's mum first. So . . . headquarters is still my room and when we're 'in the field' we use our patch under the trees at school.

I keep everything to do with Tribe in my safe. It's quite full already. There's the file with loads of fact sheets about us, a bit like Tribe Top Trumps. We're always adding new sheets. Some of them are funny, like things we did in Reception, and some of them aren't.

FUNNY THINGS TRIBERS DID IN RECEPTION

BEE: The Head told her off for talking in assembly. She shouted, 'I wasn't talking to you' – she was only four.

COPPER PIE: Walked home on his own after lunch because he didn't like the pudding.

FIFTY: Came to school with his Thomas the Tank pyjamas under his school uniform (the ones that still fit him).

> **KEENER:** Missed the whole of PE washing his hands in the loos because he'd got glue on them.
>
> **JONNO:** Held the silky label in the back of his shorts all the time because he liked the feel of it.

There's my notebook where we keep a record of everything we do – not eating and sleeping and going to the park, but important things, like when we mended the statue that Copper Pie destroyed with his catapult.

There's a paint tin to keep Tribe funds in. We all get different pocket money so everyone gives what they've got spare. We're saving up to buy things for the hut. And if we don't get the hut, we're going to have a Tribe Christmas party instead. And if we can't wait that long, we'll have a summer holiday one. Or we might just buy chocolate.

At the back, rolled up and tied with an orange and brown ribbon (Bee said it looked tribal), is a list of our rules and our manifesto. Bee wrote it. We argued about it for a while because it made us sound like we were going to change the world, and then we gave in, rolled it up and it's been there ever since.

The safe needs a five-digit code to open it. It used to be 77777 but I've changed it to 87423 – the numbers you'd press if you tried to spell TRIBE on a phone. Clever.

We do the fist of friendship whenever we meet – we

make a fist and punch each other's knuckles. It means respect. And when we leave (or when something good happens) we do the Tribe handshake. We agreed that you have to know the opening and closing actions to be part of Tribe – it's a rule. And no one knows both of them except us so no one else can join and that's good.

It would be better if Tribe was a total secret, but we told the Alley Cats and a few of them have brothers and sisters in our school so we blew it really.

It's funny how we've gone from being totally average to something special. It's actually quite annoying for two reasons . . . no, three reasons.

1. Other kids want to join. We spend ages explaining that it's not join-able. You're a Triber or you're not. And they're not.

2. Callum, who used to ignore us, is now set on making our lives difficult. He seems to think we're a threat to his position as King of the Playground.

3. As so many people are interested in us, we have to be really careful not to let anyone hear when we're talking about Tribe business.

Fifty said something yesterday that summed it all up: 'It's strange how we used to be in the middle, not liked or disliked, not unpopular but not very popular, and now we're either worshipped' (an exaggeration I thought but I'm writing down exactly what he said), 'or hated. Like Marmite.'

Bee said, 'That's what comes with fame. If you're well-known, everyone has to have an opinion about you.'

I don't think she minds being in the spotlight, but I don't like it at all. Mum says it'll die down. (Yes, I told my mum. She got suspicious because I was being so secretive and kept hiding things in my safe as she barged into my room. I think she thought I was hiding cigarettes or stuff I'd stolen. As if? This is Keener, remember?) *Well, I hope it dies down soon*, I thought. But that was before morning assembly, when it became clear that Tribe was going to be in the limelight for a while longer.

a shock
in assembly

It was whole school assembly and we were near the back, as usual, all in a line together: me, Copper Pie, Bee, Fifty and then Jonno.

The theme (there's always a theme) was sharing. There was a reading and the Year 3s did a play that was rubbish, except for my little sister Flo, who had everyone in stitches. She shouted her lines out *so* loud that everyone had to cover their ears and if anyone else hesitated, even for a second, she said their lines too. She's a nightmare.

Last of all, there were the school notices which are things like cake sales and reminders not to leave the school grounds until picked up by a parent unless you have a letter giving you permission. *Yawn!*

'We have commissioned a survey of the outside areas of

the school with a view to increasing the variety of play offered. The initial feedback suggests that, although providing a pleasant backdrop, the trees by the netball court both cast too much shade and waste valuable space that could, for example, be used as a quiet area with seating and tables.'

There was the sound of everyone in the school gasping, followed by a breeze caused by everyone turning their heads to stare at us.

'As part of our commitment to the environment, we will in turn plant some new trees along the borders by the school gates.'

What was she on about?

There was a painful few minutes of being nudged and nudging. And whispers: our den . . . no way . . . nowhere left . . . challenge the decision . . . they can't . . .

'We will consult school council which sits this Thursday, so if you have any suggestions be sure to tell your class representative.'

'Well, that's the end of you lot, isn't it?' said Callum on the way back to class. 'You'll never survive in the playground with the rest of us.'

I didn't have an answer but Jonno did. 'You don't need to worry about us, Callum. We'll stick together and of course you'll keep your eye on us.'

Callum grunted and scuttled away.

There was no chance to discuss the devastating news

until break. I suppose it gave us all time to have a think. Except Copper Pie, who doesn't believe in thinking, only action . . .

'We refuse to move. That's what we do. Sit under the trees until they agree to leave them *right where they are.*'

'It's called a "sit-in". It's what people who live in lovely thatched cottages with rose bushes do if they're bang in the way of where some horrible, greedy man wants to build a motorway,' said Bee.

'I can't see that working,' said Fifty. 'We're kids. They'd just send five big policemen with dogs to pick us up and throw us in the back of a Black Maria.'

'A what?' said Bee.

'You know, one of those mega-big police vans with blacked-out windows. So you can't see the cops beating up homeless people and drug dealers,' said Copper Pie.

'Don't be ridiculous,' said Bee. 'You watch too much of the wrong telly.'

'There's no such thing as wrong telly,' Copper Pie said back.

'Bee, you should run a school for young offenders. You'd sort them out all right,' said Jonno.

'I would too. It's common sense. Work them hard all day, outside in the fresh air doing something worthwhile, give them a big *nutritious* meal at night – homegrown organic food – and then a comfy bed. They'd be too tired and happy to commit a crime.'

BEE'S FACT FILE

- Know-all (who really does know a lot) about global warming and recycling toothpaste tubes and starving children in other countries and animal testing and E numbers.
- Is always right (she thinks).
- HATES the dark
- HATES pink
- HATES being tickled
- HATES birds

FAMILY STUFF
Twin brothers who still live at home even though they're big
Her mum LOVES shopping
Her dad HATES her mum going shopping

'They'd nick each other's food and bully the weedy ones,' said Copper Pie.

'Only if they were all like you,' said Bee.

'Shut up, you two. This is completely different from anything Tribe's faced before. We're up against the Head. It's not an equal fight so we need to be clever. We need to find a way to make the school council want to keep the playground as it is,' said Fifty, my law-abiding friend.

'But the school council is made up of geeks,' said C.P.

'And the only people who would want the trees to stay are us,' I said.

'It would help if they were nice trees,' said Jonno.

We were in trouble. Jonno didn't have any ideas either. Maybe we were going to lose our territory.

'Come on. There must be lots of eco-reasons why they should stay,' said Bee.

'Like what? The Head said they were going to plant new trees,' said Fifty.

'We can't just give up,' I said. 'We need sensible ideas.'

'Time for a brainstorm,' said Fifty.

'*Qué?*' said Bee.

'It means we all suggest things and no one's allowed to say anything bad about any of them. Mum says that knowing no one is going to laugh at what you say frees up your thinking.'

'OK, brainstorm it is. But only if no one mentions nappies, bogies or cardboard ears,' said Bee.

'You obviously don't get it, Bee. Anything goes.'

'I don't see how a list of mad ideas is going to help,' I said.

'Same,' said Copper Pie.

'Same,' said Jonno, grinning. Nobody except Fifty says 'same'.

Fifty flung his arms out and wailed, 'Why am I surrounded by idiots?'

'Same,' said Jonno, flinging his arms out.

'Same,' said Bee and Copper Pie at the same time.

144

It was quite funny, but laughing isn't the answer to *anything*.

Fifty ignored them. 'After we make a list of every possible *and* impossible solution to our problem, we go through the list and discuss them all until we find one that works.'

'Right,' I said. 'At lunch I'll bring out some paper and we'll do Fifty's brainstorm. We'll write down all the ideas and no one's allowed to criticise . . .' (Copper Pie made a you're-a-bossy-secretary face) '. . . or make faces.'

'Even if it's a lunatic idea?' said Bee.

'Even then,' I said.

'And when we've finished the list we'll go through and see which ones are any good. Understood?' Fifty said. He was starting to act like his mum. *Scary!*

Lots of nodding.

'Good. Sorted.'

It's a good job we *were* sorted because Callum wandered over.

'I thought I'd have a look around,' he said. 'See if I can come up with some suggestions for what to turn your dump into.'

Copper Pie stepped in front of him, barring his way. *Oh no! Here we go again,* I thought.

'I don't think the Head would be very pleased to hear that a Year 6 gang were blocking the way into the area she's asked us to have a look at,' said Callum.

Smarmy, bigheaded twit.

145

'It's all yours,' said Bee, smiling as she linked arms with Copper Pie and ambled into the playground.

Fifty and I followed.

'Be careful of the stag beetles,' said Jonno. 'The females have got a nasty nip.'

'Loser,' said Callum.

Jonno peered over his glasses, which is his favourite look. 'No need to be like that, Callum. I was trying to stop you from getting a bruise from some meaty mandibles.'

Jonno's so good at that. He always answers in a way that you could never say was rude or even unfriendly. He was the same when Copper Pie was trying to kill him. Always calm. Always sort of sure of himself somewhere inside, where it matters. I'm going to practise being like that.

My dear Flo, I'm very sorry that you thought I said you could borrow my remote-controlled tank. If I was going to lend it to anyone, you would be top of the list but for now it's not available for lending.

Mum, I'm sure that by asking me to be in bed, lights out, at nine you're trying to do the best for me, but I can only sleep when I feel tired and nine isn't a tired time for me. But thank you anyway.

'Miss Walsh.' Callum's hand was up the minute we walked into class. 'Miss Walsh, you know the Head told us about the tree-felling planned for the horrible corner by the netball courts?'

'Yes, Callum.'

'I've had a good idea, Miss. We could make a vegetable and herb garden and the kitchen could use the stuff we grow for our lunches.'

Someone smother him, the creep.

Unfortunately his suggestion ticked all the right boxes:

The 'improve school dinners' box,

The 'locally grown veg' box,

The 'learning where our food comes from' box,

The 'we could start a gardening club' box.

'That would be an excellent use of wasted space.' (*Wasted space? How dare she?*) 'Well done, Callum. I'll mention it to the Head.' She turned round to put Callum's name under the tick column on the blackboard.

'Excuse me, Miss, the suggestions are meant to come through the school council member, which is me,' said Lily.

Bee winked at her. She was obviously on our side.

'We can both pass on the idea then,' said Miss Walsh. 'Such an excellent idea deserves double the amount of attention.'

Doomed. Our patch was going to be overtaken by sage and parsley.

an opportunity
knocks

The brainstorm was lots of whipping wind but no roofs blown off. I don't know why but we can never have a proper talk about anything. As Bee predicted, it ended up with jokes about nappies and mashed potato. This time we got side-tracked on to what we'd take with us if we were going to sit under the trees for a week and refuse to budge from our patch (which we're not).

Lily interrupted us. 'Hi.'

'Hi.' That was Fifty.

'Hello.' That was me.

'Greetings, friend.' That was Bee.

(Lily is the only girl that Bee's friendly with. She needs at least one mate that's a girl or she'd never have a partner to do girl things with at school. Bee asked if Lily could join Tribe,

ESSENTIAL SUPPLIES FOR A SIT-IN

KEENER: Hammock, pillow, torch, books, bacon, Copper Pie (for protection).

JONNO: His glasses, binoculars, really warm socks.

FIFTY: His largest firesteel, penknife (to make kindling), pink marshmallows.

COPPER PIE: Sausages, Trumpet hidden in his sleeping bag.

BEE: Diary, air freshener (too many boys in small spaces are smelly), earplugs (in case Fifty sings), scarecrow - to stop birds landing on her when she's asleep.

but it's quite a commitment to be a proper member – you know, meetings and stuff – and your loyalties have to be to Tribe and no one else. Lily's pretty friendly with Grace so we said no.)

'I've had an idea that might help you out,' said Lily.

'Well, spill,' said Bee.

'You know I'm the class rep on the school council?'

'Yes,' we all said, keen to hear what miracle she was about to reveal.

'Well, I don't really want to be on it any more, so I

thought if I resigned and one of you took my place, you might be able to persuade the rest of the council to keep the trees and then you'd keep your den.'

'Thanks, Lily,' said Fifty. 'Nice of you to think of us. What do you think, Tribers?' He didn't sound very hopeful. I didn't feel very hopeful.

'It's bound to help having someone on the council. At the very least we'll hear what's going on before the rest of the school,' said Bee.

'Agreed,' I said.

'Same,' said Fifty.

'Is it that easy to get on?' said Jonno. 'Can you just suggest yourself?' Sometimes I forget Jonno's a new boy. He seems to have been here forever.

'No,' said Copper Pie. 'We're meant to vote people on but it's usually a fix – teachers always manage to fill the places with keeners.' He looked at me. 'Sorry, Keener. Nothing personal.' And then he looked at Lily. 'Sorry, Lily. Not your fault you get picked . . . every year.'

'Zip it, Copper Pie. You're not helping,' said Bee.

'Don't worry,' said Lily, 'I'd rather be a keener than a b— b— biffer.'

I think she was going to say 'bully' but you have to be careful. In our school it's worse than a swear word.

'I can think of a way Miss Walsh might agree to put a Triber on the council,' I said.

'Go on then, Keener,' said Jonno.

'Lily, you could say that you thought it would be nice to let Jonno have a go because he's new and it would help him settle in.'

Good idea, I thought, even though it was me who said it.

'Not a bad idea, Keener,' said Bee.

'OK. I'll try,' said Lily. 'And if it works, maybe you could persuade the council to suggest we eat our packed lunches outside again?' (We have to eat them in the canteen because of all the litter we left behind in the playground.)

'Don't see why not,' said Bee. 'But you've been on the council for ages, why didn't you ask?'

Lily bit her lip and looked upwards and sideways. 'I did, but nobody agreed with me. They all sided with Minnie who said people should eat school lunches.'

(Minnie's in the other class. She wears black stuff on her nails. Her brother's in Flo's class. They have free dinners like Bee.)

'Oh,' said Bee. 'Right. Well, I suppose we could try again?'

I nodded.

'Thanks, Lily,' said Bee.

'Yeah, thanks. Really big thanks.' Methinks Copper Pie was trying to make it up to her.

'Same,' said Fifty, smiling his toothpaste-ad smile.

'Toodle-oo,' Lily said and was gone.

'I know. I know.' Copper Pie could tell we were all about to lay in to him.

'She comes over to help and you call her a keener,' said

151

Bee. 'Honestly, Copper Pie, you're rude *and* you're stupid.'

'Steady on, Bee. He's not rude . . . only stupid,' said Fifty.

'Ha ha,' said Copper Pie.

'And how do you think you made Keener feel?' Bee wasn't giving up.

'There's a big difference between being *a keener* and being Keener,' said Copper Pie.

'Yes,' I said. 'There's no *a* in Keener.'

'OK. OK. I'm a rude, stupid . . . What did she call me?'

'Biffer,' said Bee, grinning.

'What exactly is a biffer?' I asked.

'Someone who biffs,' said Bee.

'Fine,' said Copper Pie. 'I'm a rude and stupid biffer. Satisfied?'

We all looked at each other . . . and nodded.

In English, we had to write scripts of conversations the things in our bedroom have when we're not there. I like doing things like that. I chose my bookcase, my hammock and my Deathmobile and gave them names and personalities. The bookcase was called Burp because it's too full and is always spitting out books. I called the hammock Sway (no need to explain that) and made it a daydreamer and Deathmobile was a simple killing machine – Death for short. I'd nearly finished the part where they admit how jealous they are of each other (Burp wanted to be empty, Sway wanted to be full because she can't sway without anyone lying in her and Death wanted to be liked) when Miss Walsh told us to pack up for afternoon break.

Because I wanted to finish it, I was the last one left in the classroom, apart from Lily. She repeated word for word what I'd told her to say to Miss Walsh. I waited, without breathing (but not in the I'm-going-to-faint way – I don't do that any more).

'That's very generous of you, Lily. I'm sure there are plenty of candidates for the job. And with the playground remodelling coming up, the school council has got an important job to do . . .' *Great!*

'. . . but I think we should give the class a chance to decide who takes your place.' *Not so great.*

'We'll talk about it in PSHE, last lesson.'

(PSHE is when you get to talk about non-school stuff like global warming and putting your hands over your mouth when you cough. I can't remember what the letters stand for.)

There was no need to hear any more. I shoved my books in my desk, ran out of the door, down the stairs and out through the back to our soon-to-be-flattened territory.

'Emergency,' I announced. 'Council election in PSHE, last lesson.'

'No way,' said Fifty. 'What shall we do?'

'Well, we make five votes,' said Bee. 'Let's collect some more.'

'Who are we voting for again?' asked Copper Pie.

'Jonno,' I said. 'Because he's new and no one's got a reason to not want him.'

'Except Callum,' said Jonno.

'But he's only one person. And he won't know the election's on until it's too late for him to ruin it,' said Bee. 'Come on, let's round up some support.'

Afternoon break is short. I watched Bee and Copper Pie whizzing about. Jonno stayed where he was, studying the scrub and old wood that covers the floor under the trees. I don't think he wanted to have to ask people to vote for him so he was let off. I went with Fifty and let him do the talking.

'Hi, Ed,' he said, with one of his 'special' smiles. 'Lily doesn't want to be on the school council any more so we're electing a new member this afternoon. I wondered if you'd vote for Jonno Lock because he's new, which means he has fresh ideas.'

Well done, Fifty.

'OK,' said Ed. 'Do you think he could try and get the Head to let us have our packed lunches in the playground?'

'Sure,' I said, thinking, *We'll worry about that later.*

We were going to ask someone else but we couldn't decide who, so we copped out by going to talk to Lily, who we knew would vote for Jonno anyway. The others could get the rest.

hands up
for Jonno

'Right. Today we're going to discuss why exercise is —'

'Please, Miss —' Alice asks questions *all* the time. Everyone groaned.

'No questions, Alice. All will be explained if you listen. We're going to discuss why exercise is so important.'

'Because otherwise you get fat, Miss,' shouted Callum's best friend, Jamie.

'Like Harry,' said someone from behind me.

'Who said that?' said Miss Walsh, retying the messy bun on the back of her head. She does that a hundred times a day.

No answer.

Harry's hand went up. 'Miss.'

'Yes, Harry.'

'My mum says it's puppy fat.'

'Well, she should stop feeding you it,' said Copper Pie.

Bee snorted but thankfully loads of other kids started laughing too or she'd have been for it.

'Class, that's enough. No calling out. No questions. We're going to discuss the benefits of exercise – but first we have a job to do. Lily has resigned from the school council so there is an opportunity for someone else to get involved. Would anyone like to suggest a candidate?'

Alice's hand shot up.

'But obviously you mustn't put yourself forward.'

Alice's hand dropped.

Bee had her hand straight up in the air, waiting patiently.

'Yes, Bee?'

'I'd like to suggest Jonno, Miss.'

Miss Walsh wrote *Jonno* on the board. Callum nudged Jamie, his dozy deputy, who woke up, waved his arm and shouted, 'Callum.'

'Jamie, shall we try that again?'

Jamie waved his hand and shouted 'Callum' even louder.

I giggled, and so did Copper Pie.

'No, Jamie. You put your hand up and keep it *still*, and then you wait for me to either ask you or look at you and *then* you speak because that means it's your turn.'

Jamie stopped waving. Miss Walsh looked at him – nothing. She nodded at him – he nodded back.

She sighed, wrote *Callum* on the board and drew a line between the two names.

'Good. Any more nominations or is it Jonno versus Callum?'

Silence.

'You can put your hand down now, Jamie.'

'Callum,' he shouted.

That was too much – the whole class collapsed and even Miss Walsh couldn't stop a few laughing noises escaping from her tightly pressed together teacher's lips.

'OK. Can I ask the two hopefuls to pop up to the front here? Fantastic. Now then, would either of you like to say anything about why you'd like to be on the council?'

'I will, Miss,' said Jonno.

'Go ahead then, Jonno.'

Jonno gave a little cough, pushed his glasses up his nose a bit and ran his hand through his massive mop. Each hair sprang back to exactly where it was in the first place.

'As you know, I'm new here. In some ways that's a bad thing because I don't know everything about the school, but in another way it could be a good thing. If I was lucky enough to be on the school council, I would be able to bring a fresh pair of eyes, in fact, four of them . . .' He opened his eyes really wide to make the point.

Lots of laughter.

Way to go, Jonno, I thought.

'. . . to the issues that the council is asked to discuss. Also

I've been to six schools so I can tell what worked and what didn't in other schools. And lastly, I think it would help me to settle in if I had a proper role to perform and I would be very proud to do so. Thank you.'

CLAP CLAP ROAR STAMP STAMP.

They loved it. He sounded like a real politician. It was in the bag.

'And from you, Callum?'

'If I'm elected, I will make the school better for *all* the children in it by understanding what they want and helping them get it.' He paused. 'What I *won't* do is only look out for me and my friends.'

'Thank you, Callum' said Miss Walsh, obviously a bit puzzled by what he'd said.

'Right, children. You have one vote only which is cast by raising your hand high above your head so I can easily count. Clear? Good. Votes for Jonno then, please.'

A look went round the Tribers like a Chinese whisper. Bee started it with a Callum-is-so-over face, but by the time it got round to me it had changed into a something's-gone-wrong-but-we-don't-know-what face.

There were loads of hands but in the middle of them, standing up, was Callum's dozy deputy, Jamie. 'Miss, there's something you don't know.'

I didn't panic. I mean, what was there to know?

'Jonno's friends have been bribing and threatening people in the class to get them to vote for him.'

Liar. Liar. Pants on fire.

He wasn't going to get away with that. *Someone say something.*

'That's a very serious accusation, Jamie. Jonno, is there any truth in it?'

Jonno looked shocked. 'No, Miss. I haven't asked anyone to vote for me.'

'Do any of Jonno's friends have anything to say?' It sounded like we were being tried in court.

'Yes, me,' said Fifty. 'Keener and I asked Ed and Lily, but we didn't threaten them or bribe them.'

Surely a promise about outside lunches didn't count as bribery?

Ed and Lily confirmed Fifty's statement. *Phew!*

'So perhaps I should be asking *you* what happened, Jamie?' said Miss Walsh.

He looked at Callum and then back at Miss Walsh. I tried to catch Copper Pie's eye but he was busy looking at Bee.

Even though I knew we hadn't done anything wrong, I felt uncomfortable. *Why didn't Miss Walsh send Callum and his cronies to the Head and get on with crowning Jonno and then we could get on with working out how to persuade the school council to keep the trees.*

'Copper Pie said the football team would lose their places if they didn't vote for Jonno,' the dozy deputy said.

Clearly not true.

'And Bee said if we voted for Jonno, we could have a girls-only section in the playground,' said Alice.

I couldn't believe what I was hearing. I waited for Bee and Copper Pie to stand up and declare them all filthy liars. They didn't.

'Is this true, Bee?' Miss Walsh walked over to Bee's desk. Bee screwed up her face. 'Sort of.'

Oh help!

Miss Walsh walked over to Copper Pie's desk, very slowly.

'Well?' she said.

'It's true but not right,' he said, whatever that means.

'This is extremely disappointing. Fixing the result of an election is a serious offence. Bee! Copper Pie! Off to the Head's office, I'll follow you. Class, PSHE is cancelled. I want you all to remain in your seats and read your reading books in complete silence.'

I got my book out and stared at the pages but couldn't read a single word. Talk about a mess. I felt sick. Sick because we'd ruined our chances on the school council and that meant no chance of saving our patch but more sick because we're Tribers and that means we don't lie and bribe and threaten. I thought we all understood that. What did Bee and Copper Pie think they were doing? It was like finding out that all my lovely Christmas presents hadn't come from Santa's workshop, they'd been stolen from children in an orphanage.

a pig's breakfast

After school, Jonno said he was going to wait for Bee and Copper Pie to find out what punishment the Head had given, but I pretended I had to hurry home. I didn't *want* to see them. I didn't *want* to know. I was angry with my stupid friends for making us all look bad. I didn't *want* to get Jonno elected either, if it meant we'd bullied people into it. If Jonno had tried to get votes rather than mucking about in the dirt under the trees, I bet he could have stopped the others from doing what they did. That thought made me cross with *him* too.

'Are you coming, Fifty?'

I could tell he couldn't decide whether to let me go off in a mood or tag along. He tagged along.

'What do you make of all that, then?' I asked him.

'A pig's breakfast. We'll have to find some other way of stopping the Head from stealing Tribe land for food production.'

'What?'

'I said we'll have to —'

'I heard you. I just couldn't believe what I was hearing. Don't you feel a bit . . . let down by the others? I mean Copper Pie threatened the entire football team. That wasn't the idea.'

'Well, at least he tried to get votes. We didn't, did we?'

'But Fifty. We're Tribe. We're meant to get on with people, not cheat them. We've got that rolled up paper of Bee's where she wrote all the good things Tribe were going to do.'

'It's just a name, Keener. We're five kids trying to have some fun. That's all. Don't get so worked up.'

I was so livid I could hardly speak.

'It's not just a name,' I spat out. 'We deliberately chose to be Tribe rather than a gang because people think gangs are bad. And remember what we talked about? Did it include lying and cheating?'

'No, Keener, it didn't. Look, I'm sorry, but I'm not that bothered – so they made some stuff up. Who cares?'

What was happening? I didn't want to fall out with *all* my friends.

I started to kick a stone. It was safer than carrying on the conversation.

FIFTY'S FACT FILE

- Fifty per cent as tall as everyone else (slight exaggeration)
- Black curly hair and a round face
- Loves fire
- Really loves fire
- Loves his baby sister
- Really really loves his baby sister
- Sings a lot at the wrong times
- Wants a karaoke machine
- Doesn't like disagreements
- Quick thinker

FAMILY STUFF

Dad – a postman and a wedding photographer.

Mum – bonkers, or nice and kind, depending on who you ask. She tells people what to do with their lives, like a fortune-teller.

Rose – best baby in the world!

'Look, do you want to come to mine?' asked Fifty.

I wasn't sure I wanted to, but going home didn't seem any better.

'All right.'

Now that Fifty and I are allowed to walk on our own, we

all go to each other's houses a lot more, although Fifty's is still low on the list because of his mum and no one's been to Jonno's yet.

Fifty started talking about the summer fair which was good because at least we agree about that. We're having our own stall – only Year 6s are allowed to. Top ideas are a chocolate fountain or water bombs.

We went in the back door that goes straight into the kitchen. The radio was on and Fifty's mum was sitting on a stool eating chocolate.

'Hello there.'

She stood up and gave Fifty a massive kiss and cuddle. It's gross. Thank heavens my mum doesn't do that.

'Hi Mum. Can Keener stay for tea?'

'Of course. It's puréed moles.' At least, that's what it sounded like.

'Thank you, but Mum's expecting me home for tea,' I said and followed Fifty up the stairs.

'Keener, it's time you stopped being frightened of food,' said Fifty.

I stuck my tongue out.

We played with his remote-control UFO, trying to navigate it round the obstacles in his room, and chatted about rubbish. Fifty tried to say something about Tribe but I didn't want to talk about it any more. Worse, I wasn't sure I wanted to be in it any more. A group of kids who'd trample over everyone else to get their own way. No. Not for me. I could go back to being plain Keener, that wouldn't be so bad. Or would it? That got me worrying about whether the worrying would come back. I decided to go home.

'You seem a bit quiet this evening,' said Fifty's mum when I walked back through the kitchen on my way out. 'What's bothering you?'

I was about to say, 'Nothing,' but . . .

'And don't say, "nothing",' she added.

It's really difficult not to answer his mum properly. She doesn't mind how long she has to wait. Most people find silences uncomfortable but Fifty's mum is fine with them.

'I've fallen out with Bee and Copper Pie.'

'Oh.'

One of her famous extra-long silences came next. I didn't *want* to tell her all about it but it was impossible *not* to say something. The quietness is like a vacuum – if you open your mouth it sucks stuff out of you.

I told her about the bribes and the threats. She nodded, but she didn't say anything, so I kept spewing out more and more, and she kept nodding. Eventually I ran out of stuff to moan about so I stopped talking and we looked at each other.

She sighed. 'It sounds as though Tribe is important to you.'

My turn to do the nodding.

'And you feel betrayed because not everyone feels the same as you do about it.'

165

More nodding.

'So maybe you need to talk to your fellow Tribe members —'

'Tribers. We're called Tribers.'

'So, perhaps you could talk to the Tribers —'

'But now it's ruined. I wish we'd never started it.'

'I'm sure you do, at this moment. But I don't think that's how you'll feel when you've spoken to your friends. And they have been your friends for a very long time —'

I butted in again even though it's rude. 'We were heroes when we freed the alley and now we're the baddies.'

'Goodies and baddies don't really exist. There are always several sides to a story. In fact, in my experience there are as many versions as there are witnesses. When we see something, we immediately, without thinking, use our experiences and our knowledge to understand it, so we all see something different.'

'I don't see how that helps,' I said.

'Maybe it doesn't, but before you give up on Tribe, go and talk to Bee and Copper Pie. Find out what they actually did.'

I couldn't see the point. It was quite clear they'd messed up. I didn't want to talk to them. I was fed up with talking.

I was turning the door handle to let myself out when I heard Fifty's voice – it seemed to be coming from inside the kettle. *Freaky!* He's small but not that small.

'Lickle Rose, do you want to play wiv your bruvver?'

Aha – it was coming through the baby monitor. I looked

back. Fifty's mum put her finger on her lips and grinned.

'You're the best lickle sister ever, do you know that?'

'Ba.'

'Well done, Rose. Can you say yoghurt again?'

'Ba.'

'Say yoghurt.'

'Ba ba.'

'Never mind.' A sigh. 'Tribe's falling apart. Keener thinks they did it, guilty as charged, but I'm not so sure. Maybe Copper Pie said it as a joke . . .'

A clapping noise.

'You like clapping, don't you? Or is it because I said Copper Pie's name?'

More clapping.

'Good girl, Rose. You like him, don't you? You don't think he did it.'

'Ba.'

'And maybe Bee thought it was something the council should think about. A girls-only area isn't a terrible idea.'

'Ba.'

'We need to ask them, don't we? Then we'll know why they did it.'

A burp.

'Are you windy?'

There was a moving about noise and then . . .

'MU-UM! MU-UM! Rose's been sick.'

I opened the door, gave Fifty's mum a little wave and

headed off. She was right. And so was Fifty. We needed to call an emergency meeting. It was time for the truth to come out. I could already imagine it: the Tribe Truth Trial.

the
trial

The courtroom was dark and cold. I was wearing one of those white curly wigs and a black dress. Copper Pie was in front of me, handcuffed. He had his head bowed.

'Did you or did you not threaten to leave key players out of the team if they refused to vote for Jonathon Lock as Prime Minister?'

Copper Pie didn't speak.

'Guilty,' I shouted, banging my hammer on the shiny desk in front of me.

'And did you, Beatrice Reynolds, falsely promise to turn over land for use only by girls in order to buy their votes?'

Bee climbed on to the bench in front of me and shouted, 'Save the Black Rhino.'

A policeman tried to shut her up but she shook her arms

and the chains fell off and the arms turned into wings. She flew up, grabbed Copper Pie in her talons and flew straight at me.

'Aaaargh!'

Flo landed on me and I screamed.

'Time to get up, Keener!'

For once I was glad she'd woken me up. I didn't like the dream.

'It's Friday,' she said. 'I'm going to Lucy's party the day after. I'm going to win pass-the-parcel. I asked Lucy. She said . . .'

I let her ramble on.

'. . . I want to wear silver shoes and have a handbag. I'm going to ask Amy. And lipstick.'

Mmmwa. She kissed me and disappeared to annoy Amy.

I stayed in bed for a minute, thinking about the dream. I didn't want to be the judge. It didn't feel right.

I met Fifty at the corner of my road as usual.

'I've been thinking,' I said.

'Same.'

'You first then,' I said.

'No, you go. My thinking didn't get anywhere.'

'OK.' I took a breath. 'We need to know what happened yesterday don't we?'

Fifty shrugged. 'We know what happened. Callum's lot told on Copper Pie and Bee.'

'And Bee and Copper Pie didn't deny it, did they?'

'No. That's the bit I can't work out,' said Fifty. 'It means they must have done it.'

'Maybe, but we need to find out,' I said. 'So, Tribe Truth Trial, my house, tomorrow morning.'

'Saturday morning?' Fifty was frowning. 'That's no good. Copper Pie'll be playing football.'

And I've got swimming. Stupid me. 'Afternoon then. Three o'clock?'

'Done.'

Fifty's convinced his sister has learned how to talk but pretends she can't. Ridiculous, I know. As we walked to school, we tried to devise a way of catching her out, but I was only playing along.

We bumped into Jonno by the gates.

'Hi.'

He looked pretty glum. 'Have you seen Bee or Copper Pie?'

'No,' I said.

'I waited for them for ages last night but they didn't come. The Head must have roasted them. And I didn't dare call them in case I got a parent. I mean we *were* involved.'

'Same,' said Fifty.

'Can you come over to mine tomorrow?' I asked him. 'Three o'clock.'

'What about the others?' said Jonno. 'Are they invited?'

I nodded. 'We're having a Tribe Truth Trial to sort it all

out. To find out the truth before we decide ...'

'Decide what?'

'Decide if we're ...'

I didn't want to say it. For a second I couldn't even remember what it was I was going to say.

'Keener's not impressed by what they did,' said Fifty. 'But I say let's give them a chance to defend themselves.'

I found myself saying, 'Same,' but only because Fifty had taken my words and made them his.

'You don't mean you'd give up on it? Give up on Tribe all because of Callum?' Jonno was looking at me as though I was the traitor.

'I didn't say that,' I said. 'But I know I felt ashamed yesterday.'

'Teacher's pet,' said Fifty.

I flashed him a look. Since when had all my friends been so horrible? I do *like* Miss Walsh but that's not the point.

'No,' I shouted. 'It's not that. You might think it's fine to bully everyone into doing what we want. But *I* don't.'

'Hang on, Keener,' said Jonno. 'I know what you mean. But I've been going through it in my mind and it doesn't all fit. Copper Pie may be an idiot ...'

'He's definitely an idiot,' Fifty added helpfully.

' ... but he's one of your best friends, and has been forever. And Bee ... I don't think she would do that. She manages to get her own way without needing bribes or promises.'

We nodded.

172

'So I reckon we give them a chance,' said Jonno.

'And we will, if they can explain it all away. But if not —'

Jonno got really annoyed with me when I said that. 'If not
. . . If not, what . . .? Everyone makes mistakes, you know,
Keener. Since when have you been the judge?'

Since my dream, I thought.

Fifty and Jonno were both staring at me.

'I'm not. But we can't ignore lying and —'

Fifty interrupted. 'I'm not listening to any more of this. I
thought we were loyal and equal but now Keener's the goodie
goodie and everyone else has to prove themselves. And I don't
think we should be talking behind their backs either. Let's sort
it out tomorrow.'

'But not at yours, Keener,' said Jonno. 'Let's meet somewhere neutral. It'll be fairer.'

'How about the park?' said Fifty.

'Fine. I'll tell Bee and Copper Pie. Three o'clock at the
park. For . . . What did you call it, Keener?'

'The Tribe Truth Trial,' I said quietly.

Fifty and Jonno walked off . . . without me.

BEE'S HOUSE, LATE FRIDAY NIGHT

Cast:
Bee
Bee's mum
Bee's dad
Bee's brother Patrick, older by two minutes than Luke

Patrick: Mum, you'd better come up. Bee's gone off her rocker again.
Bee's mum: That's no way to talk about your baby sister.
Patrick: Mum, she's sitting up in bed feeding ponies.
Bee's mum: Poor little thing.
Bee's mum hurries up the stairs. Bee is staring at nothing.
Bee: Not there, that's for the ponies!
Bee's mum: It's me – Mum. Are you all right, darling?
Bee: Don't get jelly on the feed.
Bee's dad comes in to see what's going on.
Bee's dad: Is she speaking in tongues again?
Bee's mum: She must have something on her mind.
Bee: This one's got a very knotty tail.
Bee's mum: Bee, do you know who I am?
Bee: Yes.
Bee's mum: Who am I, Bee?
Bee: Fish lady.

Bribes, Beetles, Bark and Bobotie

Bee's mum: Go back to sleep now, Bee.

Bee's mum strokes her head.

Bee (in a sleepy voice): Did you feed the ponies?

Bee's mum: Yes, *mia bambina*, I fed the ponies.

Bee's dad: The women in this family are all mad.

Bee's mum: Shhh. She's gone back to sleep.

hermit
crab

I've always liked hermit crabs. I think the way they carry their shells is neat and the fact that they find a bigger one when they grow is really clever. I like crows too. Jonno told me that they've learned how to get humans to crack nutshells for them so they can eat the nuts inside. They wait for the traffic lights to go red and then throw the nuts down on the zebra crossing. When the lights go green, the car wheels crush the shells and when the lights go red again, the crows go and pick them up. Neat.

Talking of zebras, Jonno told me something else. We were trying to name loads of animals that are camouflaged and Copper Pie said he reckoned zebras had to be the least camouflaged of the whole animal kingdom.

'Why make a black and white stripy creature?'

'Well . . .' said Jonno. 'It's not strictly camouflage but there is a reason.'

'Go on,' we all said.

'Zebras are easy to see when they're alone, but when they're with the rest of the herd, predators can't tell where one zebra ends and another one starts. The stripes all merge and they end up looking like a giant inedible beast rather than a hundred tasty zebras. Clever, isn't it?'

He knows loads of stuff like that. As I walked along on my own, I tried to remember some other things he'd told us. Anything was preferable to thinking about the soon-to-be-happening trial that had turned into Keener versus All the Rest of Tribe.

I thought about ringing Fifty to see if he wanted to walk with me but I wasn't sure he'd say yes. He'd probably already arranged to walk with Jonno. *Oh no!* Then I had a worse thought: *they might have all walked together.*

I wished I'd never said anything about a trial. I wished I'd waited for Copper Pie and Bee to come back from the Head's on the day of the vote and sorted it all out then. The longer it went on the worse it was. It was like a plaster stuck somewhere really hairy being peeled off agonisingly slowly rather than being ripped off in a second.

For a moment I thought how easy it would be to hold my breath . . . but Keener of Tribe doesn't do that.

Time to face up to things, I thought.

'Hi, Keener.'

I looked up and saw Fifty's black curly hair and two eyes peering at me over the high hedge that runs round the park. He was obviously standing on the platform in the play area where you wait for a turn on the pulley. A waving hand appeared next – Copper Pie's – you can tell from the browny-orange spots all over it. He clearly wasn't on the platform because that's all I could see of him.

'Get in here, Keener,' yelled Fifty.

'Are the others here?' I shouted back.

'Not yet,' said Copper Pie. 'Come on. We can all pile on together.'

Hooray! Copper Pie was:

a) talking to me,

b) willing to share a ride with me.

'Coming.' I ran round the hedge, belted through the swing gate making it clang behind me, sprinted through the sandpit and up the slope and leapt on to the base of the pulley, grabbing the rope before I landed with my feet on top of C.P.'s, nearly knocking Fifty off at the same time. With a bit of wiggling, we made room for six trainers. I hung off to one side and grinned at my two mates. Copper Pie was acting as an anchor – hanging on to the wooden post at the back of the platform to stop us drifting off before the big push.

'Ready?' said Copper Pie.

'Ready,' said Fifty.

'Ready,' I said.

Copper Pie dragged us as close to the pole as he could,

and then threw all his bodyweight against it to get the speediest launch.

Wow!

We screamed along. (Three boys are definitely faster than one.) As we hit the end, our bodies flew up so we were nearly horizontal before flopping back down and coming to a stop halfway back towards where we started.

We had a few more goes before I spotted Bee's shiny ponytail bouncing along beside the hedge, and the top of Jonno's frizzball.

Seeing all my friends together made me realise what I needed to do. I had started it so I needed to finish it. I practised in my head: *Let's not bother with the Tribe Truth Trial.* It sounded fine. We could all be friends again. I waited for everyone to stop the hellos so I could say it loud and clear . . . but then Bee told us her mad dream about a pony eating strawberry jelly and then Fifty said, 'Let's get on with it.' And then Jonno started speaking and it was already too late.

As he talked, in his oh-so-proper voice, I realised the person who deserved to be tried in a court was me. I was the disloyal one. Bee and Copper Pie may have used un-Tribe-like tactics, but I was the one that found them guilty rather than sticking up for them.

Please don't chuck me out, I thought.

'Keener,' Jonno looked directly at me. 'We've got something to tell you.'

No. Please no. I'll be better. I'll be brave and I won't mind about getting into trouble. I'm sorry. Please don't . . .

'Breathe, Keener,' said Fifty. 'Get on with it, Jonno, or he'll go weird on us.'

'We met up last night at Bee's to talk about the voting that went wrong.'

Why didn't they invite me? Shouldn't I have had a chance to explain? Why did they go to Bee's? We never go there.

'Fifty told us how you felt so we decided it might be better if you weren't there,' Jonno went on.

'But I'd like to have come. You see I've changed my —'

'Shut up and listen,' said Copper Pie. 'Get on with it, Jonno.'

'Anyway. What Callum and Jamie said wasn't one hundred per cent accurate. Turns out that when Copper Pie asked the footie boys to vote for me, they said, "What's in it for us?" So Copper Pie said, "You get to keep your place in the team." Jamie turned it round: no vote for Jonno, no place in the team, which wasn't exactly truthful. But not completely made up either.'

Bee took over. 'And I only said I *thought* Jonno would agree to *suggest* a girls-only area in exchange for votes. It wasn't definite.'

'So why didn't you tell Miss Walsh that?' I said, looking at Bee.

'Because Callum's lot didn't exactly lie,' said Jonno. I swivelled my head back to face him. 'It was close enough to

180

the truth for Bee and Copper Pie to know Miss Walsh wouldn't believe them. She's always got it in for Copper Pie.'

'*But* we managed to convince the Head, *and* we told her why we wanted someone on the council,' said Bee.

'But she kept you in the office for ages,' I said.

'Yes, but not as a punishment. The Head thought if we could study the map of the playground we'd understand how much of it is wasted by the clump of trees that we use as our patch. She said that turning it into a garden could be part of the *Go Green* project we're meant to be working on. Growing your own stuff is good for the planet.'

'So I was wrong about everything,' I said. 'Sorry.'

Would 'Sorry' be enough or had they given up on me?

'Jonno, speed up. Put him out of his misery,' said Bee.

'The thing is, Keener, we talked about it for ages —'

'Bee's mum was mad because the lasagne was getting cold,' said Fifty.

'But it still tasted fantastic,' said C.P.

'Shut up about Mum's cooking and let Jonno finish,' said Bee.

'We talked for ages and decided that in a way you were right. If your friends do things you don't agree with, you don't have to go along with them.'

Bee took over. She'd been jogging around all the time, desperate to hurry it all up. 'We decided it was a kind of braveness to stand up against us because you thought we hadn't behaved like proper Tribers.'

Copper Pie went next. 'The football team didn't get my joke, that's all. I'd never drop a good player, whatever he did – I like winning too much.'

'They didn't get the joke because ever since you kicked the goalie for letting in a lame ball they've been terrified of you.' Fifty can always be relied on to fill in the details.

'Are you ever going to let me forget that?'

'Nope.'

A feel-good wave was spreading over me.

Not expelled. Yippee!

Keener of Tribe was back.

And that meant time for my confession.

'I don't think I really behaved like a Triber either. Instead of believing Jamie and Alice, I should have at least listened to your side.'

'Don't worry, my mum never bothers,' said Copper Pie.

We all laughed. It's true. Copper Pie always gets the blame when Charlie (his brother) is around. But then, it is usually C.P.'s fault!

'And I did *nothing* to help get votes for Jonno,' I said. 'Nothing. I was too embarrassed to ask anyone to vote so I stood next to Fifty while he asked.'

'Maybe I should confess too then,' said Fifty. 'Just so that I'm not left out.'

'Too much talking,' said Copper Pie. 'Everyone was wrong. Everyone is sorry. I declare a Tribe handshake followed by all five of us on the pulley.'

'Fist of friendship first,' said Jonno. 'Rules are rules.'

We made fists and pressed our knuckles together. Then Fifty slapped his hand down and we followed: one, two, three. We didn't shout out or anything, but for me it was the best handshake ever. I was never going to risk losing my friends again. No way. Never.

Five on a pulley was tricky, but it didn't stop Bee gassing: 'One more thing. With Jonno disqualified, we might have lost the school council battle, but we've still got to save our little wooded area from the nasty woodcutter who eats people's grannies.'

'But we haven't come up with anything,' said Fifty.

'There must be something else we can do. We can't lie down and play dead while combine harvesters destroy Tribe territory,' said Copper Pie.

'Combine harvesters don't fell trees,' said Jonno.

'It's an old joke,' I said. 'Copper Pie used to call everything that wasn't a car but had wheels a combine harvester.'

'But at least I didn't have to write *R* and *L* on my hands like Fifty did,' said Copper Pie.

'Still does,' I said. My turn to be disloyal.

Fifty jumped off the platform and put his hands behind his body but we wrestled them out. Under his wrist there was a faint *R*, half washed away.

'You're for it,' said Fifty.

Copper Pie ran away pretending to be scared. Fifty chased him and the rest of us chased Fifty for no reason at all. We ran around like dogs let off the lead.

We were about to lose the corner that had been ours for ever, but we still had each other, and tribes often move on to find better food or water so we could do the same.

Tribe isn't a place. It's the Tribers.

summoning
the executioner

'I'm pleased to be able to tell you that after a flood of most original and entertaining suggestions, the school council and the staff have agreed that the wooded area of the playground will be turned into a kitchen garden, growing food to be used in the school lunches. The area will be cleared over the weekend after which Mr Morris has volunteered to take charge of fencing it off and preparing the soil for a range of delicious vegetables and herbs.'

The Head gave one of her beaming smiles that scans the room like CCTV. It's meant to make every one feel included.

We trooped out of the hall, past the statue of the school's founder, Charles Stratton, who was wearing his cardboard ear proudly. I was sure the baby elephant ear was there last

time I looked. Jonno switches them every so often and waits
for someone to notice. Last week Copper Pie stuck a sucked
barley sugar behind the good ear as a test to see if the cleaners
ever dust the statue. It's still there.

'Going to volunteer to be Mr Morris's right-hand gar-
dener, are you, Keener?'

Callum's sneery words went straight to the angry centre
of my brain.

'Might do. But don't worry, I'll leave the weeds to you.'
(Quite witty for me.) I nodded at his dozy deputy who
always follows him.

'My, my, we are getting brave now we're in a tribe.
Where's your spear and human scalp?' Callum snapped back.

Our name was bound to get back to him eventually. I
was surprised it had taken so long.

I didn't have a second clever answer.

'Those practices died out some time ago, Callum,' said
Jonno, appearing beside me. 'But we still mess with voodoo.'

Callum made his eyes mean and slitty and walked off to
class with his bodyguard.

'I didn't think it would end like this,' I said to Jonno, as
we sat down in class.

'Nor me.'

'I thought something would turn up.'

'Me too.'

'Same,' said Fifty, catching up with us.

'Oh well,' said Bee. 'I guess we can't expect to always get

186

what we want just because we've formed Tribe. We're still just five kids against everyone else.'

'It's annoying though,' I said.

'And the gardening club will never work,' said Jonno. 'We had one in my one-before-last school, but when the kids realised how long it takes to grow anything apart from mustard and cress they all gave up. They ended up more interested in the insects and worms than the courgettes and the mint.'

'So we're gonna lose our trees for an allotment that no one cares about?' said Copper Pie.

Jonno nodded.

'Well, we could still do a sit-in,' said Copper Pie.

'We could, but we don't really have a cause do we?' said Bee. 'It's not like we're saving the last elm or we've discovered an ancient silver birch or whatever. Why should anyone care, except us?'

'Bee's right,' said Fifty.

'As always,' said Bee.

We didn't bother to groan.

'So Tribe has failed,' said Fifty.

'That's enough talking now, class,' said Miss Walsh. 'I want you facing me, legs under your desks, chair legs all touching the ground.'

All through the lesson Fifty's words stayed in my ear. I didn't want to believe him, but maybe Tribe couldn't sort things out this time . . .

After school we hung around under our trees for longer than normal. It was hard to imagine the playground without the dark corner. One more day and that was it: the weekend, time for the executioner. I was worried my eyes would have trouble coping with so much sunlight having spent every break forever in the dark.

'Goodbye, my friend,' said Jonno to a piece of bark half hanging off, half attached to the trunk.

'Talking to trees now, are we?' said Fifty. 'Third sign of madness.'

'What are the first two?' asked Bee.

'Talking to yourself, then talking to my mum.'

Pretty funny, but I tried not to laugh for too long because I do quite like Fifty's mum now.

'Actually, I'm talking to this horned beetle. He's kind of a friend because I've known him since the first day here when I squatted on your land.'

'Jonno. Do us a favour – don't tell anyone you talk to insects. It's embarrassing,' said Bee.

'I don't know,' I said. 'I'd rather talk to a beetle than some people I know.'

'Same,' said Fifty. 'Come on, let's go.'

We all started trudging towards the gates. Copper Pie offered round some yellow cough sweets, but only Fifty took one. No one spoke until we reached the alley.

'Come on, Tribers, cheer up,' said Copper Pie. 'At least we saved the alley even if we couldn't save our den.'

TRIBERS' POCKETS

COPPER PIE: Cough sweets, food wrappers, string, his catapult, 13 rubber bands.

BEE: A hole.

KEENER: Phone, rubber, pencil sharpener.

JONNO: £10, door key, cloth to clean his glasses.

FIFTY: iPod, firesteel.

People murmured, 'S'pose so,' but it didn't make it any better.

At home, I went up to my room and laid in my hammock *without* a book. I had decided to make sure there was absolutely, completely, totally, utterly nothing we could do to stop the combine harvester (Copper Pie's got me saying it now) demolishing our trees.

Think laterally, I said to myself.

Nothing happened. I needed a pen and paper. It helps.

KEENER'S NOTES

- It's the Head who decides, so we need to change the Head's mind.
- The Head does what's best for the kids – supposedly.

189

> • The kids don't care whether the trees stay or not – or do they?
> • IMPORTANT! Has anyone asked them? NO.
> • The kids made suggestions for what could replace the trees NOT whether the trees should stay.
> • So if we could make the other kids want to keep the wood ...
> • How? Only Tribe want it.
> • We could offer to share ... but then it wouldn't be Tribe's any more.

That's as far as I got. I tried to imagine sharing our scrappy bit of shade but couldn't imagine anyone would want to. Except another weevil-watcher like Jonno.
THAT'S IT!!!!!!!!!!!!!
I nearly fell out of my hammock in my rush to get out of the house and round to Jonno's. We had work to do.
'Tell Mum I'm off to Jonno's. Back in a bit.'
'Fine,' said Amy.
'Hang on there,' Mum called. 'Your tea's ... blah blah —'
I'd gone. Some things are more important than tea.

at
Jonno's

I knew where Jonno lived but I'd never been inside. All I knew about his home was that it was rented and the people who owned it liked leather and glass because that's what all the furniture was made of. All I knew about his parents was that his dad thinks if you're over eight, you're a small adult. Clearly bonkers. Eight-year-olds build things with Lego. Adults build things with power tools. Eight-year-olds think poo jokes are funny. Adults don't think anything's funny. Eight-year-olds are not miniature adults, they're kids.

The door was a little bit open. Odd. I knocked anyway, but my hand accidentally made it swing open further so when a man came hurrying into the hall, I was standing there in front of him.

'Can I help you?' he said.

'I've come to see Jonno. I'm a friend from school.'

He didn't look like a dad. He was wearing all black and had long (longer than mine!) messy reddy-coloured hair and trendy glasses like Jonno's, slipping off his nose, like Jonno's do.

'And you are?'

'Keener.'

'Keener,' he repeated. 'Frances,' he called, 'come and meet Keener.'

Jonno's mum came out of the door on the left. She was wearing a long red dress, posh enough for a party. Posher than anything my mum *ever* wears, and she had her hair in hundreds of long plaits with beads on the end that clicked as she moved her head.

'So pleased to meet you . . . Keener?' She made her forehead wrinkle. 'But I don't think Keener can be your real name, can it?'

'No. But no one calls me anything else.'

'In my book that makes it real,' said Jonno's dad.

'It's very nice to meet one of Jonno's friends at last. I thought perhaps he was making you all up.' She laughed and the beads played a kind of tune.

'No, I'm definitely real . . . er . . . and so's my name,' I said. I can't usually think of anything to say when people are joking or teasing so I was quite pleased I'd come up with that.

'*Touché*,' she said. It sounded lovely but I had no idea what it meant.

'Will you be staying for supper?' the dad asked.

192

'Of course he will.' *Will I?*

'Er . . . I'd have to tell my mum.'

'I can do that for you, Keener. I haven't spoken to your mum since that day I met her in the surgery and she invited Jonno for tea. I haven't thanked you either, have I? It definitely helped him get over those new-school butterflies.' (Mums are great at saying the wrong things.)

'Thank you, Mrs Lock.'

She giggled, not in a silly way, in a nice way. 'Call me Frances.'

'Jonno's up there on the right,' the dad said. 'Go ahead, Keener.'

'Thank you, Mr Lock.'

I ran up. The door on the right was shut so I knocked.

'Come.'

I turned the handle and poked my head in.

Jonno was sitting at a huge desk with his back to me, playing something with lots of little men making lots of noise on a giant computer screen. He didn't look round – probably some critical bit that he didn't want to muck up.

'Hi,' I said.

He twisted round. He was really surprised but pleased too. I could tell by his smile.

'What are you doing here, Keener?'

'I've had an idea. And it needs you.'

'OK. I'm all ears just as soon as I destroy the Gauls with my trebuchet.'

I watched him. It was good. I'm going to get it for my birthday. You can never have too many computer games.

Finally he clicked *Yes* to *Are you sure you want to quit?*

'OK. It's about our patch. I've been trying to work out a way to save it and I think I've come up with something, or in fact, you have.'

He looked interested.

'Weevils,' I said.

'I know what they are.'

'And you know where they live,' I said. 'In our area. We launch Save the Weevils. Not Save the Trees or Save Tribe's Patch. Save the cute little insects that love dark, damp, shady places. It becomes a fight for bio . . . eco . . . green stuff . . . recycling . . . you know, Bee's sort of thing.'

He didn't say anything for ages. I waited for his verdict.

'Keener, it's awesomely brilliant. I can see it now. We can name all the creatures that thrive under the bark and on the stump. We can call it murder because they won't find anywhere else to live in the city. But . . . there's only tomorrow . . .'

'Then we'd better get working.'

Jonno ran downstairs to get some books he said we'd need. I sat on his computer chair and spun round and round. His room was fantastic. I could see loads of things to go on my birthday list: lava lamp, beanbag chair, his *own* computer and a TV – in his room!

'I'm back.'

He reversed into the room because his hands were full.

'You're so lucky. Computer in your *room*!' I said.

'Mum likes to keep me and my mess in here. She's a neat-freak.' He grinned but it didn't seem like a joke.

He plonked two massive books and one smaller one down on the desk. 'There we are, Keener. Anything and everything we need to know about weevils and beetles.'

I wasn't sure what he expected me to do. The insect bit was his department.

'Shall we write a list then?'

'I think we can do better than that. Let's get their names, the habitats they prefer, see if any of them are rare – that would be a winner – maybe get some pictures too.'

'Fine by me. But wouldn't it be quicker to use the internet?'

'Books are best.'

Jonno started flicking through, doubling back, humming and haaing, jotting down names and drawing lines between them.

'Can I have a go at your game?' I nodded at the computer.

'Sure. Log in as a guest so you don't make my army commit suicide.'

A while later, Jonno leant back and stretched his arms out. 'That should do.'

I glanced over but didn't really look. There was too much happening on the screen. 'Great,' I said.

Next thing I knew, his arm had reached over and pressed *Quit*.

'Jonno!' I was really angry. 'I was just about to —'

'This is more important.'

Not to me it wasn't. I wanted to kill the rebels and seize the loot.

'Fine,' I said. Meaning exactly the opposite.

He started talking me through all the species. It was very impressive and boring beyond belief.

MALE STAG BEETLE'S FACT FILE

- Latin name: *Lucanus servus*
- Lives in: log piles
           tree stumps
           compost heaps.
- Likes: fighting
        showing off to lady stag beetles.
- Eats: nothing at all.
- Adult only lives six months (sob).
- Not very good at flying – often bumps into things and crash lands.

'What are we going to do with all that?' I asked, looking at his sheets of tiny writing.

'I'm not sure. Make an appointment to see the Head and plead for their very survival?' He made a pleading face.

'Even better,' I said. 'Plead in Friday morning assembly in front of the *whole* school.'

'Agreed. I'll ring round – tell everyone to get to school early.'

There was a knock at the door. 'Supper's ready.'

It was a good moment for Jonno's mum (Frances!) to interrupt us. Identifying all the creatures was the easy bit, the timing was set for assembly, but how we convinced the school to save them was something else all together. Something to be sorted out tomorrow.

'What's for supper?' Jonno asked.

'Bobotie,' said his mum.

'Brilliant.'

Oh no! I had no idea what it was. Sounded runny. Could I suddenly invent a reason to go home?

There was no time. I was swished along into a dining room with a glass table and everything set for four. Two sets of glasses, serviettes: it was like a restaurant. Jonno was right about his mum being neat.

'Why don't you sit here, Keener.' She pulled the chair out slightly.

I did a recce of the table. There was a bowl of green vegetables – those peapods with nothing in the middle, broccoli and something like cabbage but much darker, a jug of water and a bottle of wine. No sign of the bootybooty or whatever she called it.

Oh, it was just arriving.

'Can you serve, Adrian?' said Jonno's mum.

His dad did my plate first. It was cat food with a thick yellow topping, like custard but solid.

'Help yourself to vegetables,' he said. I took the smallest

spoonful I could and waited because I know it's rude to start before everyone's got their food and anyway, I didn't want to eat mine.

Jonno poured everyone some water while Frances picked up the wine and filled Jonno's dad's glass and her own.

I so wished I'd gone home for tea. I couldn't eat the custard mince.

'Dig in,' said Jonno's dad.

'Thank you,' I said. And I did.

Don't ask me what happened. One minute I was sitting there thinking, *Please let a hurricane come and blow me on to an island where there are only bananas* and the next I was putting my fork in and chewing and swallowing and sipping my water and chatting (careful to speak only when my mouth wasn't full). It wasn't like talking to someone's mum and dad. It was as though a slightly older cousin was catching up with your news – one that hadn't seen you for a while. The conversation made the bootybooty go down fine.

After we'd finished, nobody leapt up like they do at mine, to escape clearing up or to get to the telly first. We all sat around, still talking.

I asked a few questions, but not as many as I wanted to. I didn't know parents could be like Jonno's.

Frances told me about the day Jonno locked himself in the car because he didn't want to go to stay with his granny. Jonno butted in and said his granny was a lunatic who made him sit for hours holding the wool for her knitting. Frances laughed and her beads made the clicky-clacky tune again. Miss Walsh was positively dull compared to Jonno's mum.

'Well, I want to catch the documentary on the abyss. Do you mind?' said the dad.

Surely he wasn't asking me?

'I might join you, Adrian. Excuse us.' She paused. 'You'll clear, won't you, Jonno?'

They left us at the table.

'Your mum's so . . .' I couldn't find the right word. *Kind? Charming?*

'Tall?' said Jonno, trying to help.

'No, that's not what I was going to say.'

'Black?'

'No! Nice . . . really nice.' It sounded a bit lame, but 'fabulous' would have made me sound weird.

'Most people look twice when they see us together. There's Dad with his red hair from his Irish side, and Mum, she looks more like my granddad who was Nigerian but now he's dead. And then me, pale skin with fair afro-hair.'

'I've never thought about it. Does that mean you're mixed race?'

'I suppose so, but that's not what I call myself – I prefer Jonno.'

'Sorry,' I said, not sure whether I'd said something wrong.

'What for? It's fine. I expect you're mixed race too.'

'Me? I don't think so. My mum and dad are from

London, and so's my nan.'

'Well, you might just be a Londoner but most people have got a bit of something else. Look at Bee.'

'What about Bee?'

Jonno realised he was going to have to give me a hint. 'Have you met her mum?'

'Yes, of course I have. Loads of times.'

'Well, she's Italian, isn't she? At least, her parents were. Why do you think she makes such lush lasagne? And Copper Pie's bright orange head comes from his Irish grandmother. Forty-six per cent of Irish people carry the red hair gene.' (*How did he know all this?*) 'So what about you, Keener? Mixed race or pure bred?'

'I'm very blond. Which countries have the most blond genes?'

'Maybe Sweden?'

I quite liked the idea of being a bit Swedish.

'Sweden. OK, I'll ask my mum and tell you tomorrow.'

While we were talking, Jonno cleared away all the dishes and put them in the dishwasher. He put a funny stopper thing on the wine, threw away the serviettes (they were paper) and wiped the table.

'Shall we go back up to my room?' he said.

'No. I've got to go.'

I really did have to go, but I had one last question. 'Why did you make your parents sound so horrible? You said they don't like children.'

200

Bribes, Beetles, Bark and Bobotie

'Well, they don't like children – at least, not the sort that climb on furniture and leave their bogies on the arms of the chairs and won't eat anything that's not with chips and tomato sauce. They like the sort that tidy away after meals, keep their rooms clean and don't talk when a documentary is on. It's hard work being the sort they like, believe me.'

Two thoughts went through my head:

1) Jonno's parents wouldn't like Copper Pie.

2) I'm so pleased I ate the bootybooty.

But I said, 'I'd better go. It's really late and it's not even the weekend.'

It was ten to nine and we had the list of endangered wildlife, but no plan except to hijack assembly. It was five of us, including three who knew nothing about it yet, against the Head, the staff, most of the kids and the combine-harvester driver. Too bad. Something would turn up. With Tribe it always did.

BREAKFAST AT JONNO'S

Frances: Keener seems very nice.

Jonno: He is.

Frances: It's great that you've made a good friend here.

Jonno: What *would* be great is if we can stay here.

Frances: There's no need to sound so angry, Jonno. Lots of families move around.

Jonno: No they don't. Keener and Fifty and Copper Pie and Bee have been friends all their lives. They've *never* moved and they're *never* moving.

Frances: Jonno, 'never' is a word you can't really trust. Who knows what will happen in the future?

Jonno: I know what will happen in my future. I'll make really good friends, like I did with Ravi, and then you and Dad will decide you don't like the . . . wallpaper, and we'll move hundreds of miles away and I'll have to start all over again.

Frances: Jonno, I won't have you talk to me like that. Perhaps these new friends of yours are not as nice as they seem if this is the behaviour you've picked up.

Jonno: Mum, perhaps it's *you* who's not as nice as you seem.

Frances: What on earth is wrong with you this morning?

Jonno: I'm fed up with being new, that's what. Fed up with no one knowing anything about me. I want a chance to hang out with old friends, not just new ones all the time. Bye. I'm off.

please let
the ground
swallow me . . .

I was standing at the back of the hall waiting for the Head to join the other staff at the front and then I was going to do it. I had a lump in my throat the size of Cyprus and my hands were shaking and, even though I'd been twice already, I still needed the loo.

I couldn't believe it when the other Tribers nominated me to do the talking. Of all of us, I'm the most useless at speaking in public. Even Copper Pie would be better, although I could see that no one would believe he wanted to save some itsy-bitsy weevils.

It was Jonno's idea. He had this theory that because I'm a goodie goodie, geek etc, I would be the most credible – that's the word he used. Fifty said it means, *inspiring trust and confidence*. That was a lot to live up to.

I was making sure I took lots of slow, deep breaths because it calms you down. *If this is calm, what's panic like?* I thought.

The double doors swung open and in marched the Head. She nodded at the school – that's the sign to sit down. I'd have given away both my sisters and all my models (even the Spitfire that hasn't made it home yet) to sit down with them but I didn't. I waited a few seconds for the fidgeting to stop and then walked through the rows of getting-smaller-nearer-the-front children and tried to ignore the disbelieving faces.

Miss Walsh was making go-and-sit-down-now-and-we'll-talk-about-it-later hand movements but I made my eyes focus on the clock behind her.

The Head is always saying that lessons and assemblies are all about taking an active part. The more the pupils get involved, the more they enjoy it and the more they learn. Not all the teachers agree – some of them go mad if there are any interruptions whatsoever, but we were banking on the Head not wanting to refuse me in front of the whole school.

'Please, Miss, I've got something I'd like to show the rest of the school. It's quite important.'

'I'm sure it can wait,' said the Head. 'Go and sit down and pop up and see me after assembly.' A fake smile followed.

'No,' I said. It came out a bit strong so I quickly added, 'Please help, it's a case of life or death.'

'It truly is,' shouted a voice I recognised from the back. *Thanks, Bee.*

'Most unusual, but, as you all know, I always welcome contributions from the children. We have got a full assembly planned out but, if it's important, I'm sure we can spare a few minutes. Hurry up then.' Her fake smile got a whole lot faker.

I turned my back to the teachers, faced the school and started to read aloud the words Jonno and Bee had written. I could feel that I'd gone the Pinky Prince colour but that was the least of my worries.

'Size is often used as a weapon. Big children pick on littler ones, large countries threaten smaller ones, large animals prey on smaller animals. There are lots of small animals that live in our playground, and probably have done for generations. I want to save those creatures from being thrown out of their homes by a larger animal, us.'

I paused and looked towards the back of the hall. The other Tribers were on their feet holding up photocopies of the *Save the Stag* poster with the list of creatures on the back that we'd made in the forty minutes between getting to school and the bell.

I carried on reading out loud but most of the audience were ignoring me and trying to see what was going on at the back. It was a shame because Jonno had found loads of good stuff about how some insects that used to be common were being driven out by the building of more roads and office blocks. I could hear a few whispers, but I couldn't tell whether anyone was on our side.

SAVE THE STAG

(AND OTHER INSECTS IN THE WOOD)

'At first me and my friends were against the clearing of the wooded area because it's where we hang out.' (Fifty said we should be honest as everyone knew that anyway.) 'But when we realised how many other species share the space, we decided to try and save it for them, not us. We didn't want to watch a . . .' (My mouth was trying to say combine harvester but my brain was trying to stop it) '. . . bulldozer kill all the insects, including the rare longhorn beetle and the endangered stag beetle.'

I'd got to the end of the speech so I walked back down through the other kids. A chant was growing, started by Bee I think, but quickly picked up by the rest.

'Save the stag. Save the stag.'

Did they really mean it? Did they want to have beetles rather than brussels sprouts and broad beans?

I looked at all the faces. They were on our side. It was fantastic. That's all it took to get the whole school on our side. I winked as I sat down with my mates. They all winked back.

'Thank you for that.' The Head put out both hands in front of her – it means, 'Settle down now or I'll get cross.'

The 'Save the stag' chant faded away.

Bee put her hand in the air. The Head could hardly ignore her, although I'm sure she wanted to. She probably wanted to expel her!

'Will you save the stag beetle or not?'

'Bee, I'm sure you realise that it's a little late to be changing the plans. Your proposal is most interesting, but I'm sure the kitchen garden will also attract many creatures. Thank you. Now I think we need to move on or morning lessons will run into lunchtime.'

She meant it as a joke but no one laughed. It wasn't funny.

I couldn't understand how she could ignore everything I'd said when it was obvious what all the kids thought. Bee must have thought the same, but (unlike me) she wasn't standing for it.

She tried to start the chanting again, faster this time. Only the kids at the back dared join in. All the little ones at the front stayed quiet. Surely the Head would have to cancel the woodcutter. Or at least postpone him.

'Save the stag. Save the stag.'

Or perhaps not.

The Head had had enough. 'We *will* have silence,' she shouted.

Everyone stopped. The Head is extremely frightening when she's angry. And she was very angry.

She turned and spoke to the other teachers. I don't know what she said. I waited. This was trouble. Would I be expelled? Mum would go berserk. I'd have to give back the phone. I'd get new-school butterflies for definite.

Miss Walsh stood up and headed straight for us. All the other teachers did the same, herding their classes out of the hall. Assembly was obviously over.

Miss Walsh pinched my arm (which Copper Pie said is assault when I told him about it later) and said, 'I wouldn't have expected this of you, Keener.'

Mr Morris went up to Bee and took the poster out of her hands before he stormed out of the hall. We were all led back to our classes and for once no one spoke. The only noise was the sound of our footsteps and some girlie crying. I was scared but I didn't want to be. We hadn't actually done anything wrong. We'd stood up for what we believe in – that's good, isn't it?

'Miss Walsh, what do you think will happen to the stag beetles?' Bee asked as soon as we got back to our classroom. She wasn't giving up. 'Will they die?'

'I expect they will find themselves another home. Insects have found ways to survive on this planet to such an extent that there are more insects than any other type of animal. I hardly think they need our help. Now, not another word from any of you. You have embarrassed me by your behaviour and gained nothing by this silly stunt.' I didn't like Miss Walsh any more. Not one bit. '6W, you will write down the spellings on the board into your books in *silence*. Thank you.'

We might have started *Save the Stag* as a stunt but the Head couldn't ignore the *whole* school supporting the campaign. Why should our views be ignored just because they'd already booked the executioner and bought the packs of sunflower seeds or rosemary or whatever? *Perhaps we should do a sit-in after all*, I thought. That would show them. My thoughts were yo-yoing between being worried about the punishment and being cross that the Head shut us all up. What about free speech?

There was a knock on the door. 'Miss Walsh, may I have a word with Keener?'

Uh-oh! What did Morris want with me? He never comes near any of us if he can help it. They wouldn't have called the police, would they? I mean, I only read the words my friends had written. I didn't mean to make everyone disobey the Head. Is there a crime called Causing a Disturbance? Could I say they'd forced me to do it?

'Take him away, Mr Morris.'

He did a come-here thing with his finger, so I stood up on wobbly legs and followed him into the corridor. I went past Bee, who made a fist. Fifty did his cut-throat sign. I avoided Copper Pie's huge feet that may or may not have been trying to trip me up and heard a very quiet 'Good luck' from Jonno as I shut the door behind me.

'Keener, might you be Flo's brother?'

'Yes,' I mumbled. It's humiliating to have a sister who's two years younger but more famous than you are.

'Bright girl. Very bright. Now, Keener, I'd like you to come down to the area you've campaigned to keep. There are a couple of interesting beasts on your very informative sheet that I'd like to verify.' He took the folded-up poster out of his jacket pocket.

Not a telling off then – I felt my shoulders drop down from somewhere near my ears to where they should be. No need to listen for sirens or to worry about what to pack for a night in the cells. But also not something I was going to be able to help with. 'We need Jonno for that, sir. I was the one who did the talking, but he's the expert.'

I stayed where I was and he poked his head back into our class and came back with Jonno.

'So you're the entomologist, are you?' Mr Morris asked him.

'Sort of,' said Jonno. 'I quite like small animals. Just because they're little doesn't mean they're simple.'

'Quite right,' said Mr Morris.

JONNO'S FACT FILE

- Knows everything about animals and people
- Is always polite to everyone
- Likes fossiling
- Hates moving house
- Would like to eat chips and tomato sauce in front of the telly to see what it's like

FAMILY STUFF
Would like a brother or sister
Dad – a consultant, earns thousands of pounds
Mum – always studying
Is treated like an adult by his parents

'Do you know an ant can work out the quickest way from *A* to *B* better than a boffin with a computer?' asked Jonno as we walked.

'Actually I did know that. But do you know how?' said Mr Morris.

They were both ignoring me, which was fine. I was beside myself with excitement – we'd found an unexpected ally.

'It uses tracks left by other ants, not footprints but chemicals that only ants recognise,' Jonno went on.

'Excellent. You know your subject, Jonno.' Mr Morris

held the back door open and me and Jonno stepped into the playground. 'So let's see what we can spot under those trees.'

Jonno and Mr Morris got down on the ground. It's wet, even in summer, and definitely dirty. No one sweeps up or anything. There's rotting wood and leaves and a tree stump – not a cut one that's flat and you could sit on, more like what's left if a tree falls over in a hurricane.

I didn't join in – too mucky.

'Yes I see, a perfect habitat in many ways.'

I don't know who Mr Morris was talking to but no one answered. The two of them crawled around looking completely idiotic for ages.

'I've read that dead wood can be a home to thousands of species,' said Jonno.

'Yes, and yet people still insist on removing decaying matter instead of seeing it as part of the natural diversity of the woodland.'

I got bored and started picking the bark when a little green shiny thing landed by me.

'I've got something.'

Jonno jumped up, Mr Morris was quite a bit slower.

'Is it a Noble Chafer?' asked Jonno.

'No. A common mistake – it's a Rose Chafer. Same family but larger.'

'Have you found anything else?' I asked.

'Several interesting finds. A longhorn, rhinoceros beetle . . . but no —'

'There!' said Jonno in a loud whisper.

Back down they went, heads over the stinky tree stump.

'So you were right,' said Mr Morris. 'Well done. Well done indeed.'

'What is it?' I asked.

'The mighty stag. One of the largest insects in Britain, and, importantly, a protected species.'

'Does that mean . . .?'

I didn't finish my sentence because Mr Morris was already nodding.

'I think a visit to the Head might be in order. I would never have agreed to be part of the kitchen garden if I'd known what a wealth of creatures were inhabiting the tree stump alone!'

Jonno held out his hand, I put mine on top.

'One, two, three.' Our hands shot up.

Mr Morris smiled. A rare thing.

'Is that some sort of clan ritual?'

'It's the Tribe handshake,' said Jonno. 'Known only to Tribers . . . and a few others.'

'Well, the secret is safe with me. Does that mean there are more of you? I noticed in the rather unorthodox assembly this morning that there were —'

'Five of us,' I said. 'There are three more.'

'Very fine. Just like the Famous Five of my youth. Well, I'll arrange a conference for morning break. Gather up your lieutenants and meet me outside the Head's office.'

'Thank you, Mr Morris,' I said.

'Thank you,' he said. 'Now, run along back to your class. I might spend a few minutes . . .'

Whatever the end of his sentence was, only the stag heard it because Mr Morris was already back down on the floor with his bum in the air.

'Like a pig snuffling for truffles,' said Jonno as we charged through the door into the corridor.

More like Probably Rose, I thought, but I didn't say it because I had something more urgent to ask. 'Have we really done it?'

'I think the answer is yes,' said Jonno, peering over his specs as usual. 'We've saved the stag.' His grin was so shiny it was like he'd had his teeth polished.

'I didn't mean the stag. I meant our patch. Have we really stopped Copper Pie's combine harvester?'

'It's the same. Saving the stag saves our patch. Saving our patch saves the stag. Everybody wins.'

'Except Callum, who won't be able to grow lettuces at Gardening Club,' I said.

'Shame,' said Jonno with a smile. 'Perhaps he could go to Dance Club instead. Learn the waltz.'

I slammed a friendly fist into Jonno's shoulder. He did the same back.

It was hell having to wait until break to tell the others. All my spellings had extra letters because I couldn't concentrate.

I kept looking at the Tribers and making big smiley faces. I even dared to do a few thumbs ups but all I got back were I-have-no-idea-what-you're-on-about looks from my mates and dissing looks from non-Tribers who could see I was either excited about something or desperate for the loo. Jonno, unbelievably but believably for Jonno (if you get what I mean), kept his head down. I know because I kept willing him to look at me so we could grin madly.

'Right, 6W. Attention on me, please. Spelling test on Monday as usual. Over the weekend I want you to write the words out three times making sure you put the *i*s and the *e*s in the right order.' She paused and looked at each Triber in turn. 'The five class members who disrupted assembly stay behind, please.'

Oh no! More waiting.

Miss Walsh stood and watched everyone troop out before she spoke. 'You may have been well meaning, but in future I suggest any bright ideas are discussed with me before being presented to the whole school. Understood?'

She looked at me, I looked down. No way was I going to nod. We'd won, she just didn't know it yet.

She looked at Bee. Bee did the smallest possible downward tilt of her chin.

Miss Walsh sighed. I think she thought we'd act a bit more sorry.

'Yes, Miss,' said Fifty, even before her eyestalks swivelled round to him.

'Jonno?'

'Yes, Miss Walsh?'

'Do you understand?'

'Yes, I understand, thank you.' He smiled at her, and pushed his glasses back up from somewhere near his nostrils.

She didn't like that. There was something about the way he said it that meant, 'I absolutely understand but it doesn't mean that I agree.'

She retied her knot of hair while she spoke. 'So, let's forget about assembly and concentrate on good behaviour for the rest of the day.'

At last! Free to talk.

'Head's office, now,' I said. 'Come on.'

'Are we in big, big trouble?' asked Fifty. 'Mum'll never agree to have a Tribe headquarters in our garden if we're in the poo.'

'No. The opposite,' said Jonno. 'Goodies through and through. Ecologically speaking.'

'Sounds too good to be true,' said Bee.

We legged it, arriving right behind Mr Morris.

'Ah! The infamous five.' He winked at us. 'Leave it to me.'

He looked down and smiled at Copper Pie's drawing of the stag beetle on our poster as though it was real.

Without waiting for an invitation, he knocked and strode in. We followed.

The Head was sitting behind her desk. 'And what can I do for you?' she said, meaning, 'GO AWAY, YOU IRRITATING KIDS, IT'S NEARLY THE WEEKEND AND I DON'T WANT ANY BOTHER.'

We didn't say a word. We didn't need to. Mr Morris told the Head all about the charismatic beetle and how its habitats were being destroyed. And more importantly, more absolutely unbelievably fantastically, he told her it was illegal to disturb them. Amazing.

Touch our patch and we'll have the law on you, I thought.

The Head looked like she wanted to mow us all down with something horrible (C.P. suggested an M4 carbine when we talked about it later), but what could she do? She didn't want to find herself on the front pages of the newspaper:

Headmistress slaughters Britain's favourite beetle against wishes of senior members of staff and junior school pupils, many of whom have suffered bad dreams as a result of the thoughtless massacre of the harmless insect.

Or in the clink.

Tribe tea
at Fifty's

School was over for the week. We decided to go to Fifty's to celebrate saving our territory from whatever vehicle, tool or weapon was meant to flatten it. I wanted to go to Jonno's so the others could see his room and meet Frances, but if we were going to build a Tribehouse in Fifty's garden, we needed to be nice to his mum, so I was overruled.

While we ate tea (lasagne – a bit runny but it went down all right), we spilled the beans about saving our patch. It was too fantastic to keep secret.

'I'm not sure what to say – it's extraordinary. Well done,' said Fifty's mum.

She was right. Everything that had happened since

Tribe began was extraordinary.

'And it'll be even better when we've got a clubhouse,' said Fifty, who was feeding Probably Rose pulverised lasagne.

'Tribehouse,' said Jonno.

'I'm not sure about your idea of building it in the garden. It's going to take a lot of work,' said Fifty's mum. 'And an adult or two!'

'My dad will help,' I said.

'And mine,' said Copper Pie.

'And we've got a plan,' said Fifty. 'I'll get it.'

He leapt up and disappeared, shouting, 'Keener, feed Probably Rose.'

Oh great!

I picked up the spoon and fed Rose the last few spoonfuls without getting too close to her.

'Probably Rose is a good eater, isn't she?' said Bee.

'Don't you think it's time you called her Rose?' said Fifty's mum.

'But Probably Rose is cute.'

'Ba,' said Rose.

Fifty came back in with a rolled-up piece of green paper and spread it out on the table. There was a picture of a house, drawn by Copper Pie, and lots of labels and arrows. It looked good.

'We can have a go, can't we, Mum?'

'Wait a minute . . . Do you want some pudding, Rose?'
she said.

'Ba.'

Fifty's mum got a banana from the fruit bowl, opened
the drawer and picked up a fork and then fetched a pink
plastic bowl. She mashed it, put the bowl on the tray of
Rose's high chair and gave me a clean spoon.

I must remember not to sit near Rose next time, I
thought.

'Right,' said Fifty's mum. 'Let's have a look at this.'
She bent over the plan.

'Dad says someone at work wants to get rid of his
shed,' said Copper Pie. 'If we take it away, we can have it.'

'Well, that would certainly help things along.'

She was going to agree, I could tell.

'Pudding,' I said to Rose, using a cheesy voice.

Rose shoved the bowl and it fell on the floor and
splattered everywhere.

'Rose!' Fifty's mum looked almost cross, even though
she says babies can't be naughty until they're two because
they don't know how.

'Sorry,' I said. The banana was all up *my* leg.

'I'll do it,' said Bee. She got some kitchen roll and
started clearing the mess up. 'You go through the plan.'
She winked at Jonno.

He took Fifty's mum through all the details. He made

it sound like we'd built hundreds of Tribehouses before.

I was listening, and paying no attention whatsoever to Probably Rose, when she poked my arm and said something like 'Yog-ert'.

I turned round so I could look straight at her. 'What did you say, Probably Rose?'

Fifty heard me. He nudged Jonno and everyone stopped talking.

'What did you say?' I said again.

'Yog-ert!' she shouted.

Fifty threw his fist in the air.

'Told you so, Keener. Told you. She can speak!'

I was too amazed to do anything . . . but Bee wasn't. She gave up smearing the banana and said, 'Probably Rose, say "banana".'

Nothing.

'OK, say "Fifty".'

Nothing. Perhaps it was just a coincidence. Perhaps 'yog ert' is another version of 'ba'.

Bee had one last try.

'Probably Rose, do *you* think we should build the Tribehouse in your garden?'

There was complete silence. We stared at Fifty's sister. She looked back at us and said, as clear as a newsreader, 'Yes.'

We all clapped. She smiled and clapped too. And then

she said, 'Yog-ert,' and pointed at the fridge.

Fifty's mum got up and fetched a strawberry and vanilla yoghurt. Before she'd finished peeling off the shiny lid, Rose had her mouth open ready for the first spoon.

'It seems Rose is in charge,' she said. 'So you'd better tell your dad to get that shed, Copper Pie. It looks as though building is about to begin.'

the Tribers
all want to say
one last thing

Bee: 'Tribe should save more things. The stag beetle was a cinch. We could try and save something bigger, more important . . .'

Fifty: 'Like a triceratops?'

Everyone started laughing.

Jonno: 'A woolly mammoth?'

Copper Pie: 'I like them.'

Keener: 'A velociraptor?'

Bee: 'Ha ha, very funny, my name's Bugs Bunny. But I bet we can find something else, maybe not an animal, maybe a special building or a person . . .'

Jonno: 'Ravi – you know, my best friend from Glasgow

– he says we should spread the word. Using the internet. He reckons that every school should have a Tribe. And we could all join together and do good things everywhere. All over the world. An army of kids.'

Fifty: 'Sounds good to me. We could have our own site and they could pay to join. We'd make a fortune.'

Copper Pie: 'There's nothing we can't do. We forced the Head to throw out the kitchen garden, didn't we? Yes, Tribe can do anything. We should take on Callum. We could make that thing you had at Jonno's . . . bootybooty, make bootybooty out of him.'

Bee: 'Or just mince.'

Fifty: 'But first we need to build our headquarters in the garden. Does anyone have a clue how to go about it?'

Keener: 'Building our HQ is definitely important but we're not meant to be making squillions from an internet business and we're not meant to be conquering the play-ground – we're Tribe, remember. What we are meant to be doing is written on that rolled up bit of paper in the safe. And it's no good going around rescuing beetles, mending statues and feeding Alley Cats if we don't do all the ordi-nary stuff too. Tribe needs to get organised or it'll be time for the summer fair and we won't get round to making the identity cards and filling up the time capsule. And what if there's another emergency? And you know, we should really have a logo . . . All important things have —'

225

Bee: 'Enough, Keener! The last word is mine. Whatever's coming next, bring it on. That's what I say. Bring it on.'

She put her hand out and four others followed.

SLAP SLAP SLAP SLAP.

'One! Two! Three! Go Tribe!'

The End
(for now)

The Tribers will soon return in a new book,
so here's a sneak peek at the next *Tribe* story!

goodbye,
Copper Pie

the school
summer fair

'Can you believe it?' said Fifty.

I shook my head.

Fifty was staring at Copper Pie, who had just blasted a ball into the top left-hand corner of the goal. He did a high five with his partner on the stall, none other than Callum – the meanest and nastiest boy in our class. In the whole school probably. The world. The universe, etc.

'Can you believe he's gone over to the dark side?'

I shook my head again. There weren't any words for how I felt.

I looked across for the hundredth time. How could Copper Pie, my oldest friend, be running a stall at the summer fair with *Callum*? Copper Pie was the one who saved me from being bitten by Annabel Ellis in nursery, the

229

one who tickled me to stop me from holding my breath and fainting in the nativity play, the one who ate my lunch every time I didn't like it.

If anyone had told me that he would desert me, desert Tribe, I'd have said they were lying. No way would he ever, ever leave: that's what I would have said. But I was wrong.

I'd been looking forward to the summer fair for ages. We all had. In Year 6, you're allowed to have your own stall. The five members of Tribe (me, Fifty, Jonno, Bee and Copper Pie) had agreed what we were doing but at the last minute Copper Pie had switched allegiance to do 'Save or Score' with Callum.

For a pound, you could choose either three shots at Callum in goal or three turns in goal trying to stop Copper Pie scoring. Their sign said, *Save three goals or score three and win a fiver.*

And to make it worse, their stall had the biggest queue. There were masses of dads and toddlers and a few girls and even some mums waiting for a turn. Every time there was a good save or an awesome shot the crowds oooh-ed and aaaaah-ed. Copper Pie was in full Manchester United strip, like Ronaldo. Callum was in a Liverpool shirt with Stevie G written on the back. I wished they weren't the centre of attention, showing off in front of the rest of Tribe. It didn't seem fair. We, the loyal ones, were doing a stall *together*, the way you should do if you're friends.

If you want to understand how I felt, imagine your mum has left you and chosen another family – a better one, tidier or funnier or better looking. Imagine watching her having a great time with them, while you stood at the side and watched.

I wanted to bang my head against something hard, except that it would hurt. I wanted to smack Copper Pie in the face and yell, but I've never hit anyone and I didn't want to start with him because he's a lot more experienced with his fists. I turned away and looked back at Fifty. He sighed. We didn't need words to know what the other one was thinking.

Bee and Jonno were sitting cross-legged under our table, talking to each other. I thought about joining them, but I didn't. I stayed where I was and watched all the people enjoying themselves.

We'd run out of things to sell on our stall. In fact we had run out twenty-two minutes after the fair started. It didn't matter – we'd made loads of money.

I thought about having a go on 'Splat the Rat'. I'm good at that. If you watch the people who go before you, you can work out how many seconds it takes the rat to slide down the pipe. When it's your turn, all you have to do is count and, when you reach the magic number, wham the stick at the space below the pipe. Everyone else waits for the rat to poke its nose out, but by then it's too late.

I decided not to have a go. I knew it wouldn't make me

feel any better. How could it? Tribe couldn't carry on without Copper Pie. I can't explain why. It's not as though he was the leader or anything – we don't have one. But he was part of its beginning and we agreed no one could leave and no one could join. So it was broken. Tribe was broken.

Will Tribe survive?
Find out in *Tribe: Goodbye, Copper Pie*
ISBN: 978 1 84812 063 1
Coming soon

Get to know
the Tribers at:

www.tribers.co.uk

www.piccadillypress.co.uk

☆ The latest news on forthcoming books

☆ Chapter previews

☆ Author biographies

☆ Fun quizzes

☆ Reader reviews

☆ Competitions and fab prizes

☆ Book features and cool downloads

☆ And much, much more . . .

Log on and check it out!

Piccadilly Press